ANCIENT ENEMY

BY MARK LUKENS

This book is dedicated to my wife, my love, who never once told me that I was wasting time writing these novels. She's the most caring person I know.

CHAPTER ONE

New Mexico Badlands

–Anasazi Dig Site

H E WAS OUT there – she was sure of it.
Stella remained perfectly still; she listened for sounds of movement around the dark room, but all she could hear was heavy breathing, some snoring, and the ceaseless wind that howled around the trailer. The room was claustrophobic with the smells of body odor, sweat, and fear. She made herself wait a few more minutes before opening her eyes. She wanted to be sure everyone else was asleep.

Under the thin sheet that covered her body, Stella was fully dressed. She even had her hiking boots on. She had been planning this for more than a day now. This was her only chance.

And David's only chance.

Finally, after counting slowly to one hundred, Stella opened her eyes just a crack. She sat up, not making a sound. She looked around the dark room at the few people who were left; some of them curled up on chairs, some on the floor. Some clutched weapons in their hands as they slept: knives, archeological axes, anything that could be used in defense.

Jake, who was supposed to be awake and on guard, slept in a fetal position on the floor, a hunting knife gripped in one hand.

Stella watched Jake as she pulled the sheet away from her body and swung her feet to the floor. Keeping her eyes on Jake, she groped in the darkness for her purse on the floor beside the couch. The keys to her rusted and battered Chevy Suburban were inside the purse.

Stella grabbed her coat from the end of the couch and stood up in the darkness. She froze. Someone coughed and snorted in their sleep, but then the person rolled over and laid still. After the four days of terror they'd been through, it was unbelievable that they could sleep at all – but the body eventually surrenders to its basic needs of food and sleep.

And survival, her mind whispered.

Stella crept past a table cluttered with labeled Anasazi artifacts that they had dug out of the cave only a week ago. Had it been only a week? It seemed like years – another lifetime. She made it to the side door of the trailer, unlocked the lock, opened the door, and slipped out into the dark night.

Jake's eyes popped open. He sat up in the darkness and watched Stella slip out the door. He gripped the hunting knife in his hand, his forearm muscles bunching. He got to his feet and walked to the back door of the trailer. He knew what he had to do.

*

Stella hurried down the trailer steps and stood on the rocky ground. Her eyes scanned the dark canyon floor – she spotted David, forty yards away, bundled up in his coat as he gazed out at the barren landscape under the starry night sky. Stella glanced back at the trailer – no one coming. Then she hurried out to David.

She stood beside David. He seemed so small and fragile, only nine years old, at least half Navajo, maybe even full-blooded, she didn't know for sure. She didn't know much about David at all; the only thing she knew about him was that the others inside the trailer wanted to kill him.

Stella touched David's shoulder, a gentle touch. He looked up at her with his dark eyes; they were almost like dark shimmering pools of liquid in the night. "David, we need to leave right now. You understand, don't you?"

David nodded. He offered her his hand. She took it and they ran.

They ran past the three temporary trailers and tents that had been set up at the dig site weeks ago. Even though they tried to be quiet, Stella could hear their shoes pounding the rocky landscape as they raced towards the group of cars and trucks in the distance. None of the vehicles worked anymore, and she wasn't sure why she believed her Suburban would start now.

But that wasn't the truth, was it? She had an idea of why her truck was going to start this time.

They were only sixty yards away from the group of trucks when Jake jumped out from behind the last trailer, the hunting knife gripped in his hand, an insane look in his eyes. His hair was wild, his clothes ripped, and he seemed to be unaffected by the freezing air. This wasn't the Jake that she'd known – longtime archeologist, longtime friend. This Jake was someone different, an animal trying to survive.

Stella and David stopped; Stella's arm shot out in front of David protectively.

"Where do you think you're going?" Jake screeched at them as he took a step towards them. "You can't leave!"

Stella didn't answer; she just watched Jake like someone would watch an unpredictable animal.

Jake took another step towards them; his eyes were unblinking orbs of terror. "You can't take him!"

"I have to," Stella answered.

"We have to do what he wants. We have to give him what he's asking for."

Stella stood her ground, her arm still in front of David. "No. I won't do this."

"We have to!"

There was a rustling in the brush near Jake. He turned and

tried to look everywhere at once. The cold night wind blew harder, it howled down into the canyon, swirling sand around, bringing the coppery smell of blood with it.

He was coming.

Jake shook his head as unnoticed tears of hopelessness slipped from his eyes. He called out to the dark night, to the dark wind. "No! I'm doing what you want!"

Stella remained in front of David, ready to protect him as best she could.

Jake backed up to the last trailer, still shaking his head no, still trying to look everywhere at once. His back touched the metal wall of the trailer and he held his knife out in a trembling hand, like it was his last line of defense.

Jake looked back at Stella, and Stella could see a realization dawning in his eyes now; she could see some of the old Jake back in those eyes. He shook his head no as tears slipped from his eyes. He tried to give her a smile, but his lips were trembling too badly. "I'm sorry," he whispered. "I can't do this anymore. I'm not going to let him take me while I'm still alive."

Stella moved in front of David to block his view of what she knew was coming next. But she wasn't able to turn away in time and she saw Jake bring the hunting knife up to his own throat. He didn't hesitate, he slashed his own throat in one sharp cut; he opened up a wide gash in his flesh that spilled dark blood immediately.

Stella turned and nudged David forward into the night, keeping him away from the horrible sight of Jake. But she couldn't block out the sounds of Jake's gurgling throat, of the liquid thump as his body hit the ground, the sound of one leg kicking at the trailer in death spasms.

"Run!" Stella yelled at David.

They bolted for the group of vehicles.

As they got closer to the vehicles, Stella could hear something chasing them, crashing through the brush – gaining on them.

The Suburban was only thirty feet away now. Twenty feet away. Ten.

Stella didn't dare turn and see what was chasing them; she opened the door of her Suburban and yelled at David. "Get in!"

David hopped inside and scrambled across the bench seat.

Stella jumped inside and slammed the door shut. Her fingers slapped at the door lock button. She rummaged in her purse for the keys to the truck. Her fingers finally curled around the keys. She tried to jab the key into the ignition with trembling fingers, but she was shaking too badly and she dropped the keys down onto the floorboard.

David sat up on his knees in the passenger seat as he stared out at the inky darkness outside the truck's windows.

Stella groped for the keys in the darkness down by her feet. Her fingers searched and searched – and then she found them. She sat back up; she didn't look at David, she didn't look out the windows, she only concentrated on getting that damn key into the ignition. They were so close now to escape – so close.

If the truck was going to start …

You know it will start this time, her mind whispered.

She managed to finally slide the key into the ignition. She twisted the key. The motor turned, it made a tired and sputtering sound. She twisted the key again; the motor cranked and cranked. Over the sound of the engine trying to fire into life, Stella could hear something outside, like the wind itself had come alive – the Dark Wind, that's what Jim Whitefeather had called it. Jim Whitefeather – the first one taken.

She couldn't think about Jim Whitefeather right now.

"Come on, damn it!" Stella screamed at her Suburban just as something slammed into the side of the truck, rocking it so hard that Stella was afraid it was going to tip over. David flew backwards and fell into the passenger door. He hit his head on the passenger window, but not hard enough to break the glass. Stella almost lost the grip on the keys, but she held onto the steering wheel and kept twisting the key.

The truck started! The powerful engine roared to life.

Stella slammed the shifter into drive. She stomped on the gas pedal. The Suburban's back tires spun in the sand and shot up a rooster tail of dirt into the night air, but the tires caught traction and the truck climbed the small, rocky incline with ease and drove up onto the dirt trail that led out of this place.

Stella muscled the steering wheel, her foot still hammered down on the gas pedal, the rear tires still spinning in the dirt – the rear end of the Suburban fishtailed, losing control. She had to be careful; she couldn't wreck the truck and leave them stranded here. With all of her will, she pulled her foot off of the gas pedal, fighting the natural urge to panic. She turned the wheel back the other way to correct their spin away from the decline back down into the parked vehicles.

She stomped the gas pedal again, and this time she guided the truck back away from the hill that they had just climbed. The truck sped up right away, the powerful engine a screaming fury again. The headlights knifed into the darkness as she navigated the twists and turns of the canyon road.

Stella let out a long breath that plumed in front of her face in the freezing air. She could breathe again – it felt like she'd been holding her breath for hours. Her muscles began to relax, her fingers loosened on the steering wheel a little.

They were safe for now.

Stella looked at David. He rubbed the back of his head, his long black hair rumpled.

"Are you okay?" she asked him.

David looked at her and nodded; his dark eyes were glassy in the night, his small breaths clouded up in front of his face.

"You're not bleeding, are you?"

David shook his head no.

Stella glanced at the rearview mirror, the dirt road barely

visible behind them in the red glow of the tail lights. But some-one stood there in the middle of the road – a man watching them leave. She was sure of it.

She looked back at David. "I won't let anything happen to you," she promised him.

David just stared at her. He didn't seem so sure.

CHAPTER TWO

Cody's Pass, Colorado

STELLA HAD DRIVEN through the night from New Mexico up into Colorado. At four thirty in the morning they reached the outskirts of the small town of Cody's Pass. Stella was bone weary, her eyes so tired it felt like she had sand in them. She saw a cheap motel at the side of the road. The vacancy sign blinked in the night.

She glanced over at David. He was still sleeping, curled up against the passenger door with his seatbelt over him. The heat was on low and the truck was warm and comfortable. She looked back at the road and pulled into the parking lot of the motel. She didn't plan on getting a room – she wanted to keep on the move. But if she could just park for an hour or two, get a little sleep.

She parked in the back of the motel, far away from other vehicles. She shut off the truck and made sure all of the doors were locked. It was still warm inside, but she figured that the creeping cold from outside would wake her up in an hour or so. She just needed to close her eyes for a moment.

Stella glanced once more at David to make sure he was still asleep, and then she closed her eyes. And she instantly slipped into dreams. Not really dreams – fragments of memories. She remembered the dig site. They had found an undiscovered Anasazi site and set up the trailers not too far away from the mouth of the small cave. Jake was excited. Stella was excited. They were finding some great artifacts, never before discovered clues to the mysteries of the Anasazi. But then Stella found David near the mouth of the cave one day. He was bloody and barely conscious. He wouldn't talk, like he was in shock. She carried him back to the trailer. She cleaned him up and asked him questions. But he wouldn't answer her, wouldn't talk at all. Jake wanted to call the police, but they were on Navajo land, with Navajo permission of course. Jim Whitefeather said he would drive to the nearest town thirty miles away and contact the tribal police. But there was something about Jim Whitefeather, something about the way he stared at David, like he was remembering an ancient story from his culture. And there was something in Jim's eyes that Stella had never seen before – fear.

And that was the day everything started happening …

Stella snapped awake, her breath caught in her throat. She looked around, forgetting for a few seconds where she was.

In my truck, her mind whispered. Parked in a … her tired mind thought for a moment, sluggish from sleep … parked in a motel parking lot.

It was cold. Stella looked at David. He was awake and staring at her with his large dark eyes.

It was still dark, but the eastern sky was beginning to lighten up with the rising sun. The sun would bring light but not much warmth to the frozen landscape. Stella turned the key and the truck fired right up. The heater blasted cold air at first, but then began to warm up.

Stella had only slept for about an hour and a half, and at first she felt worse, but she knew she would feel better soon. Even an hour and a half of sleep would help. Her mind drifted back to her dream, to Jim Whitefeather, to what happened to him. But she pushed that horror away.

She looked at David. "How long have you been awake?"

He just stared at her.

"You hungry?" she asked him.

He nodded, but still wouldn't say a word. He had spoken

only a few words since that day she'd found him. She had at least got him to tell her his name.

Stella shifted into reverse and backed out of the parking space. She pulled out onto the street and drove half a mile and saw a gas station. "We need some gas," she said, but didn't expect David to respond.

She pulled her Suburban into the gas station and parked next to one of the gas pumps. She cut the engine and stared out the windshield for a moment. "I need some coffee," she whispered. "What do you want to drink?" she asked David.

David stared at Stella, but he said nothing.

"I wish you would talk to me."

Still no answer from David.

"I know you've seen some ... some really bad things. We both have. But you need ..." She let her words trail off. Maybe she should try a different approach. "Is there someone I can call for you? Your parents? A relative?"

David stared at her, but still wouldn't respond. He looked out the passenger window.

Stella sighed and grabbed her purse. She grabbed some money; she had enough to make it through Colorado and up to her aunt's house. They'd be safe there for a little while, she hoped. They would at least get there, and then she would figure out what to do with David.

She grabbed her keys from the ignition, and flashed a smile David's way. "Come on inside with me, I'll get you a soda or something, whatever you want."

David didn't move.

Stella hesitated for a moment. She didn't want to leave David alone out here in the truck, not even for a few minutes. But she didn't want to drag a child out of her truck with people watching. "You don't want anything to drink?" she asked him.

David looked at her with his big dark eyes, but he still wouldn't answer her.

"Okay," Stella said, giving up. "I'll get something for you. I'll just be a minute. Keep all of the doors locked."

Stella got out and shut her driver's door. She'd only made it a few steps to the gas station store before she heard the sound of her truck's passenger door opening and then slamming shut. She turned and watched David as he ran across the parking lot to her. He grabbed her hand and shoved his hand into hers.

Stella could feel the sting of tears threatening, but she fought them back. "Change your mind?"

David nodded.

They entered the small store. A bell over the door dinged as they opened it. A cashier sat at the counter – she looked bored. Stella and David walked down the small aisle of groceries. David's hand was still in hers. Stella spotted a doorway that led to the restrooms. "Come on," she whispered to David. "Let's get cleaned up."

They entered the women's bathroom, then closed and locked the door. She caught a glimpse of herself in the mirror and froze for a second. That wasn't her, was it? Her hair was wild and stringy. She needed a shower. But it was her face that worried her; it was gaunt, like she'd lost twenty pounds. And the look in her eyes scared her the most. It was a haunted look, like the look in a soldier's eyes that had just come back from battle and seen horrors that he couldn't have imagined.

She washed her hands and face in the sink; she really wanted a hot shower, but this was better than nothing. She brushed her hair back with her hands and tried a smile at the mirror. Her smile seemed fake. She helped David wash up, and then they took turns going to the bathroom in the stall.

After they left the bathroom, Stella headed towards the coffee machine. She told David to go and pick out anything he wanted to eat and drink – whatever he wanted. He walked down one of the aisles of food as Stella fixed herself a cup of coffee. Just looking at the caramel colored liquid made her realize just how thirsty she was. And she realized that she was hungry. Ravenous. She spotted a warmer near the cashier's counter that held typical gas station food: pizza, chicken wings, potato wedges, fried chicken. But all they had at this time of the morning were breakfast sandwiches. Normally this kind of food would've turned her stomach, but she grabbed a few sandwiches.

Stella set the sandwiches and coffee on the counter, and then she searched the store for other supplies: bottled water, a roll of toilet paper, two toothbrushes and a travel size tube of toothpaste, a stick of deodorant, a flashlight, two bags of chips, some chewing gum. She brought the items to the counter.

"You taking a trip?" the cashier asked as she rang up the items with a methodical slowness.

"Yeah," Stella answered. "Heading up north."

The cashier met Stella's blue eyes with her own dark eyes. "I wouldn't be going anywhere right now if I was you."

Stella froze for an instant. "Why not?"

"There's a bad snowstorm coming."

The bell over the door dinged and Stella turned and saw an old man enter the store. He was dressed in overalls with a brown jacket over everything. He looked like he could be a farmer. He rubbed his hands together and stomped snow off of his boots onto the rug in front of the glass doors of the store.

Stella looked back at the cashier and slid the money to her. "We're going to make it as far as we can. I also need fifty dollars on the white Suburban out there at the pumps."

The cashier nodded.

Stella looked around for David. A sudden panic rose inside of her when she couldn't see him anywhere. She hurried down the aisles and saw him right next to the old man. David held the old man's hand, and the old man stared straight ahead with ice-blue eyes, like he was seeing something that wasn't there.

"David!" Stella yelled and rushed at the old man. She pulled the man's hand out of David's hand and stared at him. "What the hell do you think you're doing?" she asked the old farmer.

The old man shook his head like he was just waking up from a dream and didn't realize where he was. "I ... I don't know."

"You okay?" Stella asked David.

He nodded his head. She ushered David away from the old man.

The old man walked back towards the glass doors of the store.

The cashier watched him. "You don't need anything, Jed?" she asked.

"No," he said, his voice croaking a bit. "I need to get over to the bank."

Stella grabbed her bag of groceries and she and David left the store. They walked towards her Suburban, but she kept an eye on the old man as he got in his pickup truck and started it. He drove across the snow-covered streets to a bank nestled among a few other buildings along the main street. Beyond the buildings Stella could see a field of snow that stretched out for miles, there was a line of dark trees beyond the fields of snow.

She put the fifty dollars' worth of gas into her Suburban, and then got inside the truck.

Stella drove out of the gas station and parked in front of a store that looked closed. She left the engine running, left the heat blasting, and left the radio on. The radio DJ warned about the impending snowstorm.

"Yeah, we heard," Stella said to the radio.

Stella devoured her breakfast sandwich. She gave one of them to David, but he only picked at it. He ate two donuts and drank a pint of milk instead. Stella finished his sandwich for him and drank down the rest of her coffee. She bagged up the trash and threw it away in a nearby dumpster. She got back in her truck and left the door open as she brushed her teeth with some of the bottled water. She made David brush his teeth.

She felt a little better. She was full, cleaner, and calmer.

She backed out onto the snowy road as more snow began to fall from the sky. She put the truck in drive and plowed forward down the road. The town looked kind of busy for this early in the morning, like the townspeople were doing last-minute things before the snowstorm hit: gassing up vehicles, picking up food and supplies, getting money from the bank.

Stella drove towards the edge of town, but there was one more stop she needed to make first. She needed to find a payphone and make an anonymous call to the police and tell them what happened at the dig site, as much as she could tell them, as much as they would believe. Maybe a few of them at the dig site would still be alive, but she doubted that. Now that David was gone, there wouldn't be any reason for them to be kept alive. But she had to at least make the call.

When she got to her aunt's house, she would turn herself over to the police. But she wasn't going to worry about that right now. For now she needed to worry about getting David to a safe place.

She looked at David and smiled at him. "You okay?" she asked.

David stared at her and there was just the trace of a smile on his face. "Yes," he whispered to her.

CHAPTER THREE

Cody's Pass, Colorado

NOT EVEN TEN minutes after Stella left the gas station, three snowmobiles raced across the field of snow towards the main street of Cody's Pass. The snowmobiles held two men each on two of them and one man on the other one with two large metal cases strapped to the back.

Inside Cody's Pass Farmers' Trust Bank, two tellers waited on customers. Four other people waited patiently in line, snow dripping from their boots and pants. One of the customers was Jed, the old man from the gas station store.

The bank manager sat at his desk in the office right off the lobby. He shuffled through some paperwork, but there wasn't much to do – he'd already announced that they were going to be closing early due to the snowstorm, and he couldn't wait to get out of here, get home, and start his three-day weekend.

Moments later the quiet morning was shattered as the five men from the snowmobiles exploded through the front doors. They were dressed in dark coats, gloves, and ski masks; two of the men carried large metal briefcases and all of them carried guns. They moved like a military unit, fanning out in different directions. One of the masked men stayed back by the lobby doors, he locked the doors and stood guard in front of them.

Another masked man, the leader of the men, aimed his gun at the tellers as he approached them. "Nobody move!"

The tellers and customers let out short screams of shock, but they froze and watched the robbers with wide eyes.

"Open the money drawers and back away!" the leader barked at the tellers. "Don't touch anything else!"

The tellers did as they were instructed. Both of the cash drawers popped open and the tellers raised their hands as they backed away from the counter.

Another masked man, a tall and lanky man, rushed over to the customers still in line, his semi-automatic pistol aimed at them. He herded the customers to the wall. "All of you down on the floor now!"

The Leader nodded at the two men with the metal briefcases.

One of the men hopped the teller counter with ease and began emptying the money from the teller drawers into his metal briefcase.

The other man with the case rushed to the bank manager's desk, his gun trained on the man who already had his hands up, already surrendering.

"Was the alarm triggered?" the masked man yelled.

"No," the bank manager answered, shaking his head almost violently. "I ... I didn't – "

"Get up," the masked man growled at the manager. "Open the vault."

"It's already open."

"Take me there."

The masked man followed the manager behind the teller counter, around a corner to a short hall where a metal door was wide open. The manager gestured at the door with a trembling hand. "There it is."

The masked man pushed at the manager. "Get in there."

The manager's legs felt like jelly, his heart pounded so hard he thought he was going to have a heart attack. His mouth had gone so dry he could hardly spit out any words. "Please don't."

"I'm not going to kill you. Nobody's going to get hurt, I swear. As long as everyone cooperates."

The masked man's words calmed the manager down a little. He nodded and entered the vault. The masked man held his metal case open. "Fill the case up. Take from different stacks."

Back in the bank lobby, the Leader glanced down at his wristwatch. "Ninety seconds! Let's move!"

The Leader looked over at the tall lanky man who held his gun on the customers; all of the customers were on the floor except one old man who stood his ground. "What's going on over there?" The Leader growled.

The tall masked man stepped towards the old man and jabbed his weapon at him. "You hard of hearing, old man?"

The old man showed no fear of the gun pointed at his face. His ice-blue eyes had a blank look in them, like he was lost in a daydream. Or a trance. He stared at the tall masked man, but he seemed to stare right through him.

"Get down on the fucking floor!"

The old man made no move to get on the floor; he made no move of any kind. But he did smile at the masked man, his eyes still so far away, seeing something nobody else there could see. "You'd better get right with the Lord, boy," the old man said in a low voice.

"What the fuck are you babbling about?"

"You better get right with the Lord, because something real bad is coming for you."

In the vault, the bank manager stuffed stacks of cash into the masked man's metal case. "Please," the bank manager whispered. "I have a wife. Kids."

"Everything's going to be fine," the masked man told the manager. "You'll see your wife and kids again. I promise."

The other masked man with the metal case entered the vault, there was money in his metal case from the cash drawers, but there was room for much more. The bank manager stuffed his case full of stacks of money. The masked man closed the full case and handed it to his partner. "Get back out to the lobby."

The other masked man ran out of the vault with his metal case.

The masked man pointed his weapon at the bank manager who closed his eyes as tears slipped out. His lips whispered silent prayers.

"Open your eyes," the masked man growled.

The bank manager did as he was told.

"Get out in the hall, get down on the floor and just stay there. Don't follow me out, don't make a sound. Got that?"

"Yes. Yes, thank you." The bank manager hurried out of the vault and got down on the floor. He closed his eyes and he continued his whispered prayers to a God he hadn't prayed to in a long time. But he felt okay. He believed the masked man's words. Something in his voice told the manager that the man was telling the truth. He could hear the masked man walking away. "Thank you, God," the bank manager whispered. But seconds later the manager would hear gunshots and his whispered prayers would be back on his lips.

Back in the lobby, the Leader watched the old man still standing his ground as the tall masked man pointed his gun at him. "What's the problem over there?" the Leader growled.

"No problem," the tall man spat out as he glanced at the Leader, and then he looked back at the old man. "I'm only going to tell you one more time – get down on the floor!"

"The devil himself is coming for you," the old man whispered. "For all of you."

The masked man jabbed his gun at the old man. "One last chance, old man."

"I've seen what's going to happen to you," the old man whispered with a creepy smile still on his face. In a flash of movement, the old man grabbed the masked man's arm.

Suddenly, the masked man could see what the old man could see. Images flashed through the masked man's mind at lightning speed: a rustic cabin in the middle of a snowy field, puddles of blood in the snow, pieces of a dismembered body, a shadow moving down a wall.

The masked man pulled the trigger.

The back of the old man's head exploded as the bullet tore through his head, knocking him back into the wall where he slid down, leaving behind a smear of blood, his eyes still wide open, still staring right at the masked man, a ghost of a smile still on his face.

The Leader rushed over to the masked man who stood frozen as he stared down at the old man's dead body. The other customers on the floor screamed in horror and panic; they covered their heads in protection.

But the masked man only stood there, shocked by what he'd just done. He couldn't even remember squeezing the trigger.

The Leader grabbed the man's shoulder, turning him around to face him. "What the fuck are you doing?"

The masked man's eyes bulged with confusion behind the eyeholes of his ski mask, his mouth moved, trying to talk. "I ... I don't know…"

The other two masked men with the metal cases of money hurried out from behind the counters. "What the fuck happened?" one of them screamed.

The Leader turned and motioned towards the front doors where the last masked man was already unlocking them. "Let's move!"

The masked men fled the bank and ran down the sidewalk towards an alley that led to the back of the building where their three snowmobiles waited, a field of snow beyond the bank, a line of trees in the distance. They strapped the briefcases down to the back of the Leader's snowmobile, and then they hopped on the snowmobiles, two men each on two of the snowmobiles, and the Leader and briefcases on one snowmobile. They took off for the snowy field.

CHAPTER FOUR

THE THREE SNOWMOBILES raced across the snow-covered field that stretched out underneath a sky of gray clouds that promised more snow. Once they reached the cover of the unending evergreen trees, they parked and cut the engines. The world was suddenly silent around them. But not for long.

The Leader, Frank, jumped off of his snowmobile; he tore off his ski mask and marched through the snow towards the snowmobile that Jose and Needles sat on. Everything about Frank was hard and lean, his eyes were like glittering black stones set deep in a face that seemed like it was carved from granite. His dark eyes never left the two men as he raced through the snow at them.

Jose, small and twitchy, dismounted the snowmobile and stepped aside; he knew Frank was coming for Needles and he wanted to put some distance between himself and Needles right now.

Needles, a tall and wiry man, lifted up his ski mask. Prison tattoos peeked out from underneath his coat collar and wound their way up the sides of his neck. His long, unruly hair cascaded down to his shoulders. Usually Needles was an imposing figure; the kind of man you thought twice about messing with, an air of danger and violence about him. But right now he looked stunned; his eyes were wide and nervous, his mouth hung open slightly. He watched Frank march towards him.

"What the fuck, Needles?!" Frank yelled. "What the fuck happened back there?"

Needles shook his head no as he stared at Frank with lost eyes. "I don't know, Frank. That old man, he wouldn't get on the floor. He … he grabbed me. Tried to attack me."

"So you kill him?"

Needles didn't have an answer for Frank.

Frank was only a few feet away from Needles, insane fury dancing in his eyes.

Cole and Trevor dismounted their snowmobile and Cole pulled up his ski mask, revealing a handsome face and close-cropped dark hair. He rushed over and stepped in between Frank and Needles at the last second. "Come on, Frank. Let's think about this for a minute."

Frank turned to Cole – they locked eyes. Cole's muscles tensed; he was ready for anything right now. He'd seen Frank angry before, but never this angry. Finally, Frank stepped away. He paced through the snow for a moment, breathing out a long slow breath.

Cole watched Frank, still a little unsure about him for a moment. "What now, boss?"

Frank looked at Cole, then at the others. "Change of plans."

"Change of plans?" Jose yelled.

"Yes, a change of plans," Frank growled at Jose. "Since that psycho motherfucker over there decided to kill someone, every cop in the state is going to be looking for us now."

A silence blanketed them for a moment. Frank glanced at Trevor, a pale but athletic-looking man who looked more like a grad student than a bank robber. Trevor pulled out a pair of glasses from his coat pocket, completing the look. He took a folded paper out of his jacket, unfolded it, and studied it for a moment. It was a hand-drawn map. He looked up and pointed at the dark woods. "If we go through those woods for about half a mile, there will be a road."

*

Stella's rusty Chevy Suburban rumbled down the lonely

snow-covered road, walls of evergreens lined both sides of the roads; it made her feel like she was driving through a gigantic maze, a white path that twisted through big green walls. She concentrated on the road, gripping the steering wheel as the windshield wipers struggled to push the falling snow out of the way.

The heater blasted warm air at Stella and David as the radio played classic rock and roll. The song ended. "That was Fleetwood Mac," the DJ on the radio said. "Looks like there's no end in sight for the big series of snowstorms moving through. Some areas can expect at least another foot of snow and possible whiteout conditions."

"Yeah, we know," Stella muttered at the radio.

Stella watched the road, slowing down a little as they rounded a curve which revealed more trees. More and more trees. Unending trees. No buildings. No other cars in sight. No signs of human life. She hadn't seen another vehicle for the last twenty minutes. That was probably because everybody else knew about the snowstorm; they were already tucked safely inside their homes, ready to ride out the storm. They weren't driving through it like idiots.

She glanced at David who stared out the windshield, his body rigid, his face tense. He looked out the passenger window and watched the dark green blur of trees whip by, then he turned around and stared out the back window of the Suburban, watching the road and dark trees disappear into a mist of white snow.

Stella forced a smile – hopefully a reassuring smile. "David, don't worry. It didn't follow us."

David turned and stared at Stella with his dark eyes, searching her eyes for the truth.

Stella smiled and changed the subject. "Don't you want to know where we're going?"

David nodded. "Where?" he whispered.

"My aunt's house. She lives in northern Colorado. We'll be

safe up there. I promise. Then we'll figure out what to do next. We'll call someone for you."

David looked down at his coat and toyed with one of the buttons.

Stella watched the road for a moment as she rounded a bend. She glanced back at David as she talked to him. "There has to be someone I can call for you."

No answer from David.

"David, why won't you tell me?"

Still no answer from David.

"You need to talk to me," she said a little louder and sharper than she had intended.

David looked at Stella. His eyes drilled into hers, they seemed to burn into her mind for a split second. "My parents aren't here anymore."

The words shocked Stella. "What do you mean? What happened to them?"

David looked out the windshield, his eyes widened in shock. "Look out!!"

Stella looked back at the road and saw a man dressed in a dark coat standing in the middle of the snow-covered road; he waved his arms, trying to flag her down. She stomped her foot on the brake. Too hard. The tires locked up; the Suburban skidded along the snow and ice, sliding helplessly.

"Hold on!" Stella shouted at David as she muscled the steering wheel, trying to turn the truck, watching in horror as the man only stood there, perhaps frozen with fear. The truck got closer and closer to the man, and then it slid right past him, barely missing him.

Her truck slid off the side of the road and ran down through a ditch where it crashed through snow drifts and shrubs, running some of the shrubs over, crunching them to the ground, before finally coming to a stop with a jolt.

Stella sat there for a moment in shock; her fingers gripped

the steering wheel like she was still driving. The windshield wipers thumped back and forth, the headlights stabbed through the murky daylight, one of the headlight beams at a crazy angle now.

For a moment Stella's mind buzzed with panic. It was him, her mind whispered, it was the person she'd seen standing in the road when they'd left the dig site. But her rational mind fought back. It wasn't the same person. She'd seen the man's face for a split second as she slid past him.

She turned to David. "Are you okay?"

David nodded as a shudder of breath escaped him, his eyes still wide with shock.

Stella looked back out the windshield as she exhaled a long breath. "What ... who was – "

A rapping at her driver's window cut her words off, a small scream escaped her throat. She turned and stared straight into Cole's ruggedly handsome face.

"Are you okay?" Cole called through the driver's window. He bent down, his face close to the glass, his breath coming out in plumes, fogging the glass a little.

Stella nodded as she rolled down the window; the freezing air invaded the truck immediately. "Yeah, we're okay. What were you doing in the middle of the road? Is something wrong?"

Cole winced as he pulled his pistol out from his coat pocket. "I'm sorry, lady." He pointed the gun at her. "We need your vehicle."

CHAPTER FIVE

STELLA COULDN'T MOVE or respond; she could only stare at the barrel of Cole's gun pointed at her face.

Cole backed up a few steps, his boots sinking down into the snow piled up on the side of the road. He looked across the road, but his pistol was still aimed right at Stella.

Stella's eyes darted to the other robbers who emerged from the trees; they crossed the empty road, they looked like black blurry shapes at first in the snowy mist, but in a moment they crystallized into human beings, criminals with scowls on their faces, metal briefcases and guns clutched in their gloved hands.

Cole looked back at Stella. "Just take it easy. We're not going to hurt you. We just need a ride."

Stella nodded, her hands still on the steering wheel, still gripping it without realizing it.

"Slide over," Cole told her.

Stella pried her hands loose and slid across the bench seat without a word; she slid right up next to David.

Cole looked at Frank. "We need to get this thing back up on the road." He shoved his gun inside his coat pocket and plopped down in the driver's seat, he adjusted the seat back quickly. He shifted the Suburban into drive, his foot down on the brake, snow dripping all over the floorboard.

Frank opened the back door and threw one of the metal cases of money inside. He turned to Jose who held the other metal case. "Throw it inside, Jose," Frank growled at him.

Jose threw the metal case inside, it clunked against the other case.

"Get back there and help them push," Frank told Jose.

Jose sighed, but he hurried to the back of the truck, joining Trevor and Needles.

Frank waited by the open back door, his hands on the door and the frame of the truck, ready to help push. "We're ready!" he called out to Cole.

Cole closed the driver's door and lifted his foot from the brake and pressed gently on the gas pedal.

The tires spun; snow spit out of the back, pelting Trevor, Jose, and Needles as they pushed. They dug their boots into the snow, trying to find a purchase in the snow.

The tires spun and spun as the men strained, grunting and growling, muscles burning. Cole gave it a little more gas. The engine revved, and the tires suddenly grabbed, gained traction, and inched back up onto the road. The three men let go of the Suburban as it climbed back onto the road. They were breathing hard, hands on their hips.

A crashing noise through the trees caught their attention. All three men reached for their guns, ready to aim and fire. All three men stared into the thick woods – but they couldn't see anything moving among the trees.

"What the hell was that?" Needles asked with true fear in his voice.

The noise was gone now.

"Maybe it was a bear," Jose said.

"Bears should be hibernating this time of year," Trevor informed him as he put his gun away.

"Then some deer," Jose said. "How the fuck do I know?"

Jose and Trevor ran to catch up to the Suburban as it waited on the road, its powerful motor rumbling, exhaust pluming up from the tailpipe, the tail lights bright red dots in the murky day, the increasing clouds making the day even darker and drearier.

Needles stared into the dark woods as fear crept into his body. That wasn't a deer in the woods, he knew that. It was something bad in there. Something bad coming for all of them.

"Needles!" Frank yelled from the Suburban. "Hurry the fuck up, or I swear to God we're going to leave you here."

Needles tore his eyes away from the trees and hurried to the waiting truck.

As Needles got in the backseat of the truck, Frank blocked Jose from getting in the other side. "No room in here," Frank told him. "Get in the back."

"Why the hell do I have to get in the back? Tell Needles to – "

"Just get in the fucking back," Frank growled at him and stared daggers at him.

"Alright. Fuck, man."

Cole found the latch for the hatch and pulled on it, and he heard the clunk of a latch in the back opening.

Frank sat down in the backseat and slammed the door shut as Jose hurried to the back of the truck.

As Jose ran to the back of the truck, a moment of panic seized him – he was sure that Cole was going to stomp the gas pedal and take off, leaving him here alone on this desolate road in the middle of a blizzard. But the truck waited. Jose pulled the hatch up and crawled inside, and then he pulled the hatch door closed against the snow and biting wind. It wasn't exactly warm inside the Suburban, but it was a lot warmer than outside.

Jose tried to get comfortable on top of the piles of tools scattered around the back of the Suburban; there were tarps, shovels, picks and other digging tools. He moved to the back seat and propped his hands and head over the back of the seat in between Trevor and Needles, but he stared at the front of the truck. "What are you?" Jose asked Stella. "A gravedigger?"

Stella glanced back at Jose, and then she turned back around and stared out the windshield. "Something like that," she muttered.

Cole gave Stella an odd look, but he didn't say anything.

Trevor looked at Jose who was right beside his face now. "You mind sitting back a little?"

Jose smiled at him, inches away from his face. "Why? Is this bothering you?"

"Your breath is bothering me."

Cole shifted into drive, and then stomped down on the gas pedal; the truck slid sideways on the road before finally gaining traction.

Jose, not ready for the sudden jolt forward, fell over in the back of the truck and smacked his elbow on a shovel. "What the fuck?" he called out. "You trying to run us off the road again?"

Cole just smiled.

"Shut the fuck up back there," Frank growled. He glanced back at Jose, but then he watched Needles. Needles stared straight ahead, but it was like he wasn't seeing anything, like he was lost in some different world. There was something wrong with Needles, Frank was sure of that now. But he couldn't worry about that at this moment. Right now, they had more pressing issues. Like this woman and this child.

Cole concentrated on the road. He was an expert driver, and he maneuvered the large truck around the bends and curves of the road much faster than Stella would've dared. "This storm is getting worse," Cole said to no one in particular.

The music on the radio was interrupted by the DJ, back with an announcement. "We've received some breaking news. Police are on the lookout for five men wanted for a bank robbery earlier today in Cody's Pass where one man was shot and killed. Police are asking – "

Cole clicked off the radio.

The truck was silent except for the growling engine, thumping windshield wipers, and howling wind.

Cole looked at Stella as he drove. Stella looked right back at Cole, matching his stare, holding it, showing no fear of him.

David stared out the passenger window, lost in thought, watching the unending trees whip by in a blur. It was like he never even heard the radio broadcast. But he'd heard it, Stella was sure of that.

Frank leaned forward from the backseat and tapped Stella on the shoulder.

Stella jumped from the touch, like a current of electricity had just jolted her. She spun around and stared at Frank.

"What's your name?" Frank asked, trying what he thought was a reassuring smile – but it wasn't working.

"Stella."

"Okay, Stella. Don't worry about anything. Nothing's going to happen as long as you stay cool. We just need to get to the state line, find another vehicle. Then you can have your truck back and be on your way."

Stella nodded. But she didn't believe a word Frank was saying. She turned back around without a word.

"Aw hell," Cole said as he glanced down at the instrument panel.

Everyone in back leaned forward. "What is it?" Frank asked.

Cole shook his head in disbelief. "The engine's overheating."

CHAPTER SIX

EVERYONE IN THE truck leaned forward – except David, who still seemed to be in his own world.

Frank gripped the back of the driver's seat as he leaned his head forward. "What the fuck are you talking about, Cole?"

"The engine's overheating. She must've punctured the radiator when she ran this truck off the road."

"Yeah, to avoid hitting you," Stella muttered.

Cole ignored Stella's comment as he glanced down at the temperature gauge; the needle was already climbing into the red. He glanced out the windshield and he could see steam drifting up from under the hood, blending in with the swirling snow. "We need to find somewhere to stop or this motor's going to seize up."

Trevor leaned forward even more and pointed at the windshield. "Look. I think I see a mailbox."

Cole drove on for a few more seconds and he could see a mailbox on the side of the road materializing out of the snowstorm. He eased down on the brake pedal, slowing the large SUV down to make the turn. They turned at the mailbox onto a narrow drive that was cut through the dense trees. The truck bumped along the rutted trail as tree branches scraped along the windows and sides of the truck.

Everyone was tense and quiet as Cole navigated the twists and turns of the driveway that seemed to be going on forever through these trees.

"How long *is* this driveway?" Jose asked from the back.

"If this is even a driveway," Trevor muttered.

Cole kept glancing down at the temperature gauge; it was in the red now. The steam poured out of the front of the truck like a ghostly mist rushing at the windshield. They weren't going to make it much farther, Cole thought to himself, but he didn't want to say the words aloud.

After one more bend in the drive, the trees gave way to a large open field, acres of cleared land in the middle of the never-ending forest. And only a few hundred yards away was a log cabin.

Cole smiled as he drove across the field of snow (which he hoped was still a driveway) to the front of the cabin, he turned the truck so that the headlights shined on the dark cabin thirty yards away, and then he shut the motor off. Everything was quiet now except for the howling wind of the storm. Steam drifted up in a cloud in front of the truck for a few seconds, obscuring their view of the cabin, but then the wind blew the steam away and they could see the cabin in the glow of the headlights.

The cabin was dark, no lights on inside, no smoke drifting up from the chimney. To the right of the cabin was a large, free-standing garage with a pickup truck parked in front of it. The pickup truck sat under a blanket of snow – it looked like the truck hadn't moved in a while.

"I don't believe this. It's fucking freezing out here and the engine's overheating," Jose said, and again he poked his head in between Trevor and Needles.

"Ironic, isn't it?" Trevor smiled at Jose.

"Whatever you say, man,"

Cole stared at the cabin in the glow of the headlights; he watched the curtains in the two windows underneath the roof of the front porch which ran the length of the front of the cabin, there was no movement of the curtains, no one peeking out from the dark rooms of the cabin. His eyes flicked to the door. It remained shut.

"Can this truck be fixed?" Frank asked Cole.

"Maybe. If we're lucky it's just a hole in one of the hoses."

They sat in silence for another moment, all of them staring at the dark cabin.

"Maybe no one's home," Trevor finally said.

"Only one way to find out," Frank said and opened his door into the howling wind. He got out and ran through the snowstorm to the front porch of the cabin. Jose and Trevor didn't waste any time, they followed Frank out into the storm – Jose had to crawl over the backseat to get out.

David opened the door, ready to get out. Stella touched his arm gently. They locked eyes for a moment, but David turned away and got out of the truck. Stella grabbed her purse, she was about to follow David, but Cole grabbed her arm. She turned and stared at Cole.

"We're going to knock on the door," Cole told her. "Don't try anything stupid. Okay?"

Stella just nodded, and then she ripped her arm out of Cole's grasp; she got out of the truck and hurried after David.

Cole looked back at Needles who still waited in the backseat, staring at the cabin in horror.

"You coming?" Cole asked Needles.

Even though Needles seemed afraid of this place, he couldn't tear his eyes away from it. "This place," he whispered. "Something's wrong here. Really, really wrong."

"Needles!" Cole barked, and Needles finally tore his eyes away from the cabin and looked at him. "Needles, you better get your shit together. You hear me? You're the reason we're here in the middle of fucking nowhere instead of at the warehouse splitting the money up."

"But Cole, you don't understand – "

"Just get it together."

Cole got out of the truck without another word to Needles.

Cole and Needles met up with the others on the front porch.

Frank stood in front of the solid wood front door, he had already slipped one of his gloves off, and he pounded on the door with his fist.

They waited. No answer at the door.

Trevor watched the window to the left of the door – no movement of the curtains inside, no lights turning on inside.

Frank pounded on the door again.

Trevor walked to the window and cupped his hands beside his face and peered in through the glass.

"See anything?" Cole asked.

"Naw," Trevor answered. "Too dark." Trevor tried to open the window, he lifted up, but it wouldn't budge.

Frank tried the door handle. He jiggled it, but it was locked. He looked at Trevor. "Go around back and check it out."

Trevor hurried across the front porch and hopped the railing with one quick movement; he landed down in the snow, turned the corner and disappeared around the side of the house.

*

Trevor hurried down the side of the house, his boots sinking into the snow that reached up to his knees in some places. He reached the corner of the cabin and peeked around to the back of the cabin. Nothing much back here: a small stack of firewood against the back wall of the cabin; a wheelbarrow overturned and buried under snow; a small wood building that looked like it housed a water pump or well. Trevor shielded his eyes as best he could from the stinging snow and walked towards the back door of the cabin set in the wall of logs.

He climbed the steps up to the door and tried the door handle. Locked.

He turned and looked out at the field that stretched out from the back of the cabin. The field in the back of the cabin was at least three times the size of the field in the front. He was about to head back to the front of the cabin when he thought he caught some kind of movement out of the corner of his eye in the field.

He looked back out at the field, at the line of trees just barely visible in the distance through the snowstorm.

Nothing there. No one moving. No animal moving.

Again, he was about to go back to the front of the cabin, but then he heard a clicking noise from the back door; the noise was audible even over the howling wind. He looked at the back door as it slowly creaked open.

"What the fuck?" Trevor whispered. He pulled out his Glock nine millimeter from the waistband of his pants and crept towards the back door. He walked up the steps and stood in the doorway and stared at the darkness inside the cabin. It took a moment for his eyes to adjust to the darkness, but then he could see a hallway that led away from the doorway he stood in. He could make out closed doors along the hall, two on one side, and one on the other. The hallway at the other end opened up to what seemed like a living room, but the living room was too dark to make out much detail.

Trevor hesitated for another moment in the doorway, his gun gripped in one gloved hand. The wind of the storm howled behind him, some of the snow even drifted inside the doorway onto the wood-planked hallway floor.

"Hello?" Trevor called out.

No answer.

"Is someone here?" Trevor waited for another few seconds. No answer. No sounds of any kind coming from inside the cabin. "Our car is overheating. We need to use a phone." Trevor took a step forward; the floorboards creaked under his weight. His eyes were beginning to adjust even more to the darkness now.

"Hello?" Trevor called out again as he took another few steps. He didn't like this – something felt strange here, wrong. He was afraid some old man would be waiting in the darkness with a shotgun, praying for the day some punk would try and break into his cabin. But there was something else he was afraid of, something much worse, a deeper fear, like a fear from a long time ago when he was a child – the fear of a monster in the closet, a monster in the darkness, something unimaginable waiting for him.

Trevor took one more step forward and that's when the back door slammed shut.

CHAPTER SEVEN

COLE, STELLA, DAVID, and the others waited on the front porch as the snowstorm scattered snow across the floorboards of the porch.

Cole glanced at both ends of the front porch. What was taking Trevor so long?

Jose hugged his arms, shivering. "Maybe nobody's here right now. Maybe this is like a summer cabin or something."

Frank had his back to the cabin as he stood at the edge of the porch in front of the steps; he stared out at the vast field in front of them, the line of dark trees just barely visible through the swirling snow. Frank's face was as hard as stone as he stared at the trees, he didn't move a muscle; and finally he answered Jose. "Maybe."

Needles stood by the railing of the front porch, almost leaning against it, like he didn't want to be close to this cabin. He stared at the cabin with that same look of terror Cole had seen in his eyes when they were sitting inside Stella's Suburban.

Frank's eyes, like little black stones, noticed Needles. "What the hell's wrong with you?"

Needles shook his head in disbelief. "This can't be right," he muttered.

Frank was about to ask Needles what the hell he was talking about when the front door of the cabin flew open.

Both Frank and Cole drew their guns and aimed them at the front door, only a split second away from pulling the trigger.

Trevor stood in the doorway, a big smile on his face. "The place is empty."

Cole lowered his gun and let out a breath. "That's a good way of getting yourself shot, little brother," he said.

Frank glared at everyone else. "Come on, let's get inside."

Jose walked up behind Stella and pushed her towards the door. "You heard the man, get inside."

Stella whirled around on Jose. She stared at him with piercing blue eyes – she showed no fear of him. "I can walk by myself."

Jose took a step back without even realizing it.

Stella turned to David and took one of his hands. "Come on, honey. Let's get out of the cold."

After they were all inside the cabin, Cole closed and locked the front door, then he twisted a deadbolt lock shut. He turned and looked around at the cabin, which was really one big room, a living room and a kitchen divided by a half wall and dining room table in between. The hallway led off from near the dining room table to the back door and bedrooms and a bathroom.

The décor was rustic, masculine; it didn't seem to have a woman's touch. A couch took up nearly one wall of the living room, a blanket thrown over the back of it. A recliner sat near the couch, closer to the hallway – the two pieces of furniture didn't match. A large TV occupied the corner closer to one of the front windows; it was the only really modern-looking thing in the whole cabin. Between the TV and couch was the fireplace, cold and gray now, but charred marks suggested a recent fire. A stack of firewood sat on the large stone hearth, an ax leaned against the stone fireplace. Other fireplace tools dangled in a stand on the other side of the fireplace screen. Cole gazed up at the high, vaulted ceiling. He could hear the wind howling through the eaves outside.

Stella and David stood in the middle of the living room on a woven Native American rug that consisted of bright colors and strange designs. The snow dripped off from their shoes and dampened the middle of the rug.

Frank nodded at Stella and David. "Go sit on the couch for now."

Stella and David did as they were told; they sat down on the couch right next to each other. David took one of Stella's hands in both of his and they watched the men huddle together in the middle of the living room. Except Needles, he didn't huddle; he stumbled over to the dining room table and plopped down in a chair like his legs had suddenly gone weak.

Jose hugged his arms. "It's cold in here, man." He spotted a thermostat on the wall near the hallway and hurried over to it. He moved the dial and listened for a moment. He heard a slight click. He looked at the others, a big smile on his face as the heat kicked on. "We've got electricity here. We got heat."

Cole looked at Trevor. "How'd you get inside?"

"It was weird. I tried the back door, and at first I thought it was locked. It seemed like it was locked. I was about to leave, but then the door opened."

"What do you mean, it opened?" Cole asked.

Trevor shrugged. "I don't know. I guess it must've been stuck or something."

Cole didn't say anything, but something about the back door being unlocked bothered him. The windows and the front door were locked, but the back door had been left unlocked?

And something else bothered Cole. He stared at the kitchen beyond the dining room table. A refrigerator and some counters took up one side of the kitchen. A sink, stove, and more counters on the other side. A large freezer sat on the floor at the far wall of the kitchen. There were two frying pans on the stove. A few unopened cans of food sat on the counter. A sink full of dishes. Cole nodded at the kitchen. "Look at the kitchen. Somebody was in here not too long ago."

Frank glanced at Cole, then the kitchen, then back at Cole

and Trevor. "You guys check this place out. Make sure no one's hiding back there."

Cole and Trevor hurried down the hall. As Trevor went to check out the second bedroom, Cole entered the small bathroom. He saw a tub with the shower curtain drawn shut, toilet, sink, mirror above the sink, small window on the far wall by the toilet, snow piled up on the window sill outside. There were a few small Western pictures hung up on the walls, a threadbare rug on the floor in front of the tub.

Cole caught a glimpse of himself in the mirror: his chiseled face, his short hair which was spikey now from the melting snow glistening in it. But his eyes stopped him, his dark eyes that looked so tired. He just wanted this job to be over. And it would've been over by now if Needles hadn't killed that old man in the bank.

Cole opened up the medicine cabinet. Normal stuff inside: cough medicine, shaving cream, cheap razors and cologne, a stick of deodorant. He reached inside and pulled out a prescription bottle of medicine, some kind of antibiotic. He shook the container, only a few pills rattled around inside. He read the name on the bottle – Tom Gordon.

He set the pills back inside and shut the mirrored door. Cole knew someone lived here, this wasn't a seasonal cabin or a hunting lodge – this was someone's home. And that someone had just been here not too long ago. But where was that someone now? Where was Tom Gordon?

Cole looked down at the sink. The faucet dripped water into the basin. He turned the water on for a second, and then turned it off. He turned the handle as hard as he could, but the water still dripped.

Cole left the bathroom and went to check out the other bedroom.

*

In the living room, Frank stared at Needles who still sat at the dining room table. Needles still had a frightened look in his eyes as he stared around at the cabin in disbelief. Frank pulled out a chair and sat down next to Needles, watching him the whole time. "You okay, Needles?"

Needles didn't answer Frank.

Frank leaned towards Needles, speaking to him again, his voice sharper, louder. "Needles!"

Needles turned and stared at Frank for a long moment, his expression miserable, his eyes lost in some other world. "I didn't mean to shoot that old man in the bank. I swear I didn't. It was an accident. You know me, Frank."

Frank nodded. "I know."

Needles pulled out a crucifix on a chain from under his thermal shirt as he looked away from Frank. He rubbed the cross gently over and over again with his fingers – a nervous habit. "This place," Needles said in a low voice. "I've seen it before."

This caught Frank off guard. "What the hell are you talking about?"

Needles turned and faced Frank, his rheumy blue eyes boring into Frank's coal-black eyes. "When that old man grabbed me in the bank, I saw things. Bad things. I saw this place."

Frank inhaled a deep breath; he let it out slowly, trying to calm himself. This was the last thing he needed – Needles taking a nose dive off the edge of sanity. "Needles, just take it easy. I know you're still upset about what happened."

"Upset?!" Needles screamed at Frank. He jumped up from his chair and jabbed a finger at Frank. "You don't understand what the fuck's going on here!"

CHAPTER EIGHT

COLE ENTERED TOM Gordon's bedroom; he walked around the bed, which wasn't made, and he scanned the room with his eyes. There were books and magazines stacked up against one wall. A pile of dirty clothes near a closet door, a flannel shirt and T-shirt draped over a chair. An old TV, one of those big heavy ones, sat in the corner on top of a scratched and scarred table.

Cole found the remote control to the TV on the night stand next to the bed; the remote was lying right beside a Louis L'Amour book: The Haunted Mesa, which was open and face down, a place being saved in the book. He pressed the power button on the remote and turned the TV on, but there was only static. He switched through channel after channel – only static. He shut the TV off and tried the telephone next to the bed; it was one of those older telephones that made an annoying ringing sound when someone called. There was no dial tone. He checked to make sure the phone line was plugged in. He jiggled the hang-up buttons – still no dial tone. He ripped the cord out of the wall, unhooked it from the phone and balled up the cord in his hands.

Phone lines must be down from the storm, he thought. Maybe the TV, too. But the electric was still on. The water was still on. Those were good things. Cole stood at the foot of the bed a moment longer, staring down at the messy bed. He bent down and looked underneath the bed. No Tom Gordon hiding there. No Tom Gordon in any of the closets.

If this Tom Gordon wasn't here in the cabin somewhere, then

he'd left in a hurry just before they got here. But what would make someone leave so suddenly in the middle of a snowstorm?

A small dark spot on the carpet near the foot of the bed caught Cole's attention. He bent down and touched the spot on the carpet – sticky, a little wet. He brought his finger up to his face to inspect the red liquid on his finger tip. Blood? It sure looked like it.

Trevor entered the bedroom and Cole quickly wiped the blood from his finger. "All clear in the other room," Trevor said. "How about this room?"

"No one here," Cole said.

The yelling from out in the living room caught their attention; Frank and Needles were screaming at each other out there. They hurried back out to the living room. "Everything okay out here?" Cole asked.

Frank glared at Cole and Trevor, and then he looked at Needles. "Sit the fuck down, Needles."

Needles remained standing at the dining room table, his finger still pointed at Frank, his hand trembling. For a moment Frank thought Needles was going to yell again, start babbling again, but Needles sat back down without another word, he looked down at the table as he rubbed the crucifix around his neck with his fingers.

Frank's eyes darted over to Stella and David who sat on the couch, David still held Stella's hand and he stared at Frank with his large dark eyes. Frank looked away from David, to Needles. He had to get Needles back in line, get this whole thing under control. "That's right, Needles," Frank said. "Just calm down. We all need to stay calm."

Needles looked at Frank, a bead of sweat trickled down the side of Needles' forehead despite the chilly air. His face twisted into a tortured mask and he seemed to be on the verge of tears. "You don't understand, Frank. We can't stay here. We're all going to die. I've already seen it."

Frank pointed his finger at Needles and glared at him with murderous eyes. "Not another fucking word – you hear me, Needles?"

Frank walked away – he needed to get away from Needles for a moment.

Cole glanced at Needles who went back to rubbing the crucifix around his neck, whispering something to himself, a prayer perhaps, and then Cole followed Frank into the kitchen. Cole set the balled-up telephone cord on the kitchen counter as Frank opened the refrigerator, checking the food supply.

"Nobody in the back rooms, but someone definitely lives here. Someone named Tom Gordon. I think he lives here alone."

Frank looked up from the refrigerator, their eyes locking for a moment.

"I found a prescription pill bottle with his name on it." Cole looked over at the stove, at the two frying pans on the burners, at the couple of cans of food waiting to be opened. "It's like this guy was just here. Like he was just about to make some lunch, then he suddenly left."

Frank closed the refrigerator door. "You should've been a fucking detective. Maybe this guy forgot something. Went to the store."

"This guy's kitchen is stocked for the winter. And why would he leave when a blizzard is moving in?"

"Maybe he saw us pull up and he took off out the back door."

Cole nodded. "But there would've been footprints in the snow; the storm wouldn't have covered them up that quickly. And leaving on foot? I don't think this guy would've panicked just because someone pulled up in his front yard."

Frank glanced at the freezer against the wall as Cole continued. "And this house was cold when we got here. No lights on. No heat on."

"You said you thought this guy just left," Frank said.

"It seemed like he left suddenly, but it must've been a little while since he was here."

Frank shook his head, like this was beginning to give him a headache.

"I think we should move that lady's truck around to the back of the cabin in case this guy comes back," Cole said. "Get it out of sight."

Frank thought this over for a moment, and then nodded. "Yeah. You and Trevor move the truck around back. And bring those cases inside."

Cole hurried over to Trevor. "Come on, let's go."

Cole unlocked the deadbolt, and then opened the door up to the howling snowstorm. Cole stepped out onto the porch. Trevor was about to follow him, but Jose called out to him. "Bundle up, sweetie."

Trevor flipped Jose a middle finger. "Fuck you," he muttered and rushed out onto the porch and slammed the door shut.

Frank watched the door for a moment, and then he looked at Stella and David. Frank walked over to Jose. He leaned in close to Jose as he spoke in a low voice. "Go out there and watch those two. If they try and run, kill them."

*

Cole and Trevor got inside Stella's Suburban. Cole started the truck and the temperature gauge climbed immediately into the red. He shifted into drive and gunned the gas. He needed to get this truck behind the cabin before the motor seized up halfway there.

As Cole drove, Trevor lit a cigarette with his Zippo lighter. The cabin was just a dark blur to their right – that's how much the blizzard had intensified.

Once the truck was safely out of view from the driveway, Cole put the truck in park and shut the engine and headlights off. He sat there for a moment as Trevor inhaled on his cigarette and blew out smoke. Cole stared at his little brother.

Trevor looked at Cole. "I know what you're going to say, Cole. I'm sorry. I didn't know all of this was going to happen."

Cole sighed as Trevor took another drag off his cigarette. "It was supposed to be a simple job," Trevor continued. "But that fucking trigger-happy Needles fucked everything up."

"When we're out of here," Cole said, "you give Frank what you owe him and we're done with this. Okay?"

"Yeah."

"Swear to me, Trevor."

"Yes, Cole. I promise." Trevor took another drag from his cigarette. He looked at Cole again, trying to change the subject. "What do you think's going on here?"

"I don't know. Something isn't right here."

"What about Needles?"

"I think he's losing his fucking mind."

Trevor just nodded.

"Come on," Cole told Trevor. "Let's get those cases inside."

Cole and Trevor got out of the SUV. They opened the back door and grabbed the cases of money. They turned and saw Jose standing in the snow, just watching them.

"What are you doing out here?" Cole asked. He was ready to reach for his weapon. He knew what could happen on big jobs like this, when there was so much money at stake. People got greedy. People wanted more than their share. And sometimes those people were ready to kill for it.

"Frank sent me out here to help you," Jose said.

"Help us with two cases?" Cole asked, the howling wind trying to tear his words out of the air.

Trevor tossed his case of money at Jose. "Be my guest."

CHAPTER NINE

THE FRONT DOOR burst open. Cole, Trevor, and Jose stomped inside the cabin as snow dripped from their coats and boots. Trevor slammed the door shut and locked the deadbolt.

"Where do you want these cases?" Jose asked.

"Set them over there by the fireplace," Frank growled at them.

Jose and Cole set the dripping metal cases on the hearth right in front of the small pile of cut wood and the large ax. Cole turned and gave Frank a sarcastic grin. "This good, boss?"

Frank didn't answer Cole.

Trevor shrugged off his coat and threw it over the back of one of the dining room chairs. "What now, boss?"

Frank stared at Stella and David. "I think it's time we asked this lady some questions."

Frank walked across the room to the couch and stood in front of Stella and David. "Stella," Frank asked in a calm voice that seemed menacing no matter how nice he tried to make it sound. "You got a cellphone on you?"

Stella shook her head no.

"Let me see your purse."

"I told you, I don't have a phone."

Frank held his hand out, waiting for her to hand the purse over.

Stella sighed and handed Frank her purse. Frank tossed the purse to Jose. "Check it out."

Jose dumped out the contents of Stella's purse onto the dining room table. He moved the items around: a wallet with a driver's license and a few credit cards inside, a pack of gum, a brush, lip balm, scraps of paper. He picked up the wallet and read the driver's license as he looked at Frank. "Stella Weaver from Arizona wasn't lying. No phone in here."

Frank turned back to Stella. "Where were you two headed?"

"A relative's house. My aunt's house."

"Far from here?"

"Northern Colorado."

"So she's expecting you?"

"No, it was going to be a surprise."

Frank's eyes moved to David. Frank crouched down in front of David, trying to get on the kid's eye level. Frank smiled at the kid, it was supposed to be a comforting smile, but it came across as menacing. "Hey, kid. What's your name?"

David didn't answer, he just stared at Frank.

"His name is David," Stella answered.

"I was talking to him," Frank told her with his eyes still on David.

"He doesn't talk much," Stella said. "Especially when he's scared."

Frank nodded and stood back up. He glared at Stella. "Where were you two coming from? What's with all the tools in the back of your truck?"

"I'm an archeologist. I specialize in Southwest American Indian cultures, especially the Anasazi. They were a people who used to live in what is now the Southwestern United States until they mysteriously vanished around – "

"Enough with the history lesson – where were you coming from?"

"We were coming from a dig site in New Mexico."

"And David is your son?"

Stella hesitated. "Yes."

"No he's not."

Jose left the contents of Stella's purse scattered all over the table. He walked into the kitchen and rummaged through the cabinets.

Cole walked to the dining room table and collected the contents and put them back into Stella's purse.

Jose moved boxes and cans around in one of the cabinets, and then he broke out in a big smile. He pulled out a nearly full bottle of whiskey. "Jackpot," he whispered.

Cole brought Stella's purse back to her and handed it to her. As she took it, he asked her a question. "Who are you running from?"

The question caught Stella by surprise. She took her purse and set it on the couch beside her. "What do you mean?" she finally asked. "I'm not running from anyone."

"There aren't any bags or suitcases in your truck," Cole said. "Not even a change of clothes. Only some items you bought at a convenience store."

In the kitchen, Jose closed the cabinets and walked over to the large freezer against the far wall. He lifted up the lid of the freezer, expecting to see pieces of wrapped meat. What he saw made him stumble back a step, the freezer lid slammed shut with a thump.

The others turned at the noise of the lid closing.

Jose turned and looked at them with shock in his eyes. "You guys better come take a look at this."

CHAPTER TEN

COLE, FRANK, JOSE, and Trevor gathered around the freezer, it was a tight squeeze in the small kitchen. Even Needles broke out of his daze and stood up at the dining room table, staring at the others in the kitchen. But he wouldn't enter the kitchen. "What is it?" he asked. "What's in there?"

Nobody answered Needles. They all stared down at the freezer.

"I guess we know where Tom Gordon is now," Cole finally said.

Stuffed inside the freezer was Tom Gordon's body, his legs and arms bent at odd angles, like his limbs had been broken when he'd been stuffed down inside. He looked like some doll stuffed down inside a kid's toy box. Except that this doll didn't have any eyes – Tom Gordon's eyes had been carved out.

No, Cole thought, they didn't seem like they were carved out – they looked more like they were torn out of his face.

Or eaten out, his mind whispered.

"Holy shit," Jose muttered. "Holy shit, I can't believe this. What the fuck, man?"

Stella and David still sat on the couch; David's hands still clutched one of Stella's hands. She looked at David and their eyes met. Stella felt a lump in her throat, a knot of dread worming its way through her body. She had promised David that it hadn't followed them. She had promised him that it wouldn't be able to find them. She had promised David that they would be safe now.

But the look in David's eyes stung her. He had dared to believe her. But now he knew the truth. It had found them.

Needles hurried over to the kitchen, rushing up behind the others. "What did you find in there?" he asked, his voice trembling.

Jose turned and marched away from the freezer, needing to pace, needing to move, needing to be away from the gory sight of Tom Gordon's body.

Needles walked to the freezer on unsteady legs. He took Jose's spot. He stared down at the body and inhaled a sharp breath, and then it was like he couldn't exhale, like the breath was caught in his lungs.

"Shit," Frank finally said as he stared down at Tom Gordon's crooked body. The lips of Tom Gordon's mouth were pulled back in some kind of strange rictus smile. There were two deep black holes where his eyes used to be, ragged gray flesh around the edges. But there was no blood anywhere on his face, or anywhere around him.

"Somebody was in here," Jose rambled, still pacing back and forth by the dining room table. "Somebody was in this fucking cabin and they killed that guy. Stuffed him in the fucking freezer. Took his fucking eyes out."

Needles could finally breathe again. He stared at Frank. "I told you, Frank. I told you we couldn't stay here. There's something bad here. There's something coming for us. For all of us."

"Shut up, Needles," Frank growled.

"The devil's coming for us. That's what that old man in the bank said. The devil's coming for us and he's going to kill us all."

"I said shut up," Frank snapped. "I'm trying to think."

Cole watched as Needles backed away out of the kitchen, shaking his head no over and over again. "No, I'm not staying here. I'm not waiting for the devil to come."

Frank rushed at Needles and grabbed him by the front of his thermal shirt, his fists bunched up in the fabric. He pushed

Needles back a few steps into the kitchen counter. "You want to leave so bad?!" he yelled at Needles, spittle flying from his lips. "Go on, then!"

Needles stared at Frank for a long moment, his body trembling; his eyes darted to the front door like he was re-thinking his statement, like he was thinking about being out there alone.

"Okay, then," Frank said as he let Needles go. He turned and walked away. "Just shut up and let me think."

Everyone was silent, the cabin eerily quiet except for the non-stop howling wind outside. Jose couldn't take the silence anymore. "We need to do something, man. There's some kind of psycho running around out there."

Frank looked at Jose. "There's nothing we can do right now while that blizzard's out there. We're stuck here for the night."

"What about that guy's truck parked out there?" Jose asked. "Maybe it runs. Maybe we should start it up."

"In the morning," Frank growled. "After the storm lets up."

Cole looked back down into the freezer at Tom Gordon's body; he studied it for a moment. Then he turned and opened a drawer near the stove. He rummaged through the kitchen utensils until he found a long wooden spoon. He poked Tom Gordon's body with the spoon's handle. The handle of the spoon pushed into Tom Gordon's soft flesh. "Somebody did this to him within the last few hours," Cole said. "His body isn't even frozen yet."

"Oh, that's comforting," Jose snorted.

Trevor looked around. "This doesn't make any sense. There should be blood all over the place. His eyes are gone. There should be blood somewhere."

Cole thought of the large single drop of blood he'd seen in the bedroom, but then decided against saying anything about it. It was only one drop of blood; Trevor was right, there should be a hell of a lot more blood somewhere in this cabin. He looked at the others. "No signs of struggle anywhere in the cabin."

"Maybe they knocked the guy out," Frank suggested. "Then carved out his eyes and stuffed him in the freezer."

"Why?" Jose asked as he walked back towards the group. "Why would someone do that?"

"I don't think it was a robbery," Cole answered. "It doesn't look like anything was taken. It doesn't even look like anything was searched through."

"Then why, Sherlock?" Jose asked. "Someone just killed this guy for the hell of it. Just for shits and giggles?"

"Maybe he had some enemies," Trevor said. "Maybe he owed someone some money." Trevor and Frank locked eyes for the briefest of moments.

"Then this place would've been ransacked," Cole answered quickly. "They would've looked for the money in here."

"Then it's some fucking psycho," Jose said. "Some psycho who just likes to kill." Jose glanced at the front door of the cabin. "Maybe he's still out there. Maybe he saw us pull up here in front of the cabin."

Stella and David stood up from the couch and started to walk towards the hallway until Frank's voice stopped them in their tracks.

"Where the hell do you think you're going?"

Stella stared at Frank. "We're going to the bathroom," she answered in a strong voice.

"Both of you?"

"There might be a crazy person out there. I'm not letting David out of my sight."

Frank sighed and made a go-ahead gesture. He turned back to the others.

Cole glanced at the hall. He waited until he heard the bathroom door close and lock. A thought occurred to him, a thought he didn't want to say aloud. Maybe whoever Stella and David were running from did this to Tom Gordon.

*

Stella closed and locked the bathroom door. She looked at David.

"It's happening again," David whispered; his voice trembled as he stared up at her with his dark eyes.

Stella nodded. "I know."

"You said we would be safe," he whispered to her. "You said it wasn't going to follow us."

A pang of guilt ran through Stella. "I know. I'm sorry."

"It's going to start asking for things," David said, his voice getting louder.

"Sssh," Stella said as she glanced at the bathroom door, and then she looked back at David, locking eyes with him. "David, listen to me. This is very important. I know you're scared. I'm scared too. But we have to be strong. We can't let them know what we know. Do you understand?"

David just stared at her.

"We can't let them know that we've seen this before. We have to try and survive. You know what's going to happen at first. We have to be patient and plan a way out of this. Just like last time. Okay?"

David finally nodded.

"Can you be strong?"

David nodded. "I'll try."

"Good," she said. She got down on one knee and hugged him, holding his trembling body tight. "I'm going to protect you again. I swear I will. You believe me, don't you?"

David nodded as she held him. "Yes," he said into her shoulder.

Stella and David both jumped from a sudden loud knocking at the bathroom door. "Let's not make a career out of this in there," they heard Jose say from the other side of the door.

Stella and David looked at each other. "A career?" Stella said, and she couldn't help it – she burst out laughing. David began to laugh a little, but Stella couldn't stop. It wasn't even funny, but that made it somehow funnier in her mind.

Finally, they regained their composure. Stella flushed the toilet to make it seem like they had used it. Then she washed her face in the sink and then she washed David's face with the warm water and a wash cloth. "We're going to be okay," she whispered to him. "We're going to get through this. I promise."

*

They all watched Stella and David as they came out of the bathroom and walked back to the couch and sat down. Stella stared at Frank. Frank could see something different in her eyes – defiance, a lack of fear.

Frank finally tore his eyes away from Stella. He turned to Trevor. "Find some blankets and sheets. Pillows. Sleeping bags. Anything you can find. We're all sleeping out here in the living room together where we can keep an eye on each other."

Trevor took off down the hall for the bedrooms.

Frank looked at Cole. "Tomorrow, when the storm lets up, you check out Stella's truck – see if it can be fixed."

Cole nodded.

"Check out that other truck out there, too. And the garage. Maybe you can use some parts from that truck on Stella's truck."

Cole shrugged, but he didn't look too hopeful. "Yeah, maybe."

Trevor came back with an armload of blankets, sheets, and pillows. He dumped them on the floor, but he kicked a blue sleeping bag away from the blankets and sheets. "I got dibs on the sleeping bag," he called out to everyone.

"We'll sleep in watches tonight," Frank said. "I'll take the first watch."

CHAPTER ELEVEN

COLE'S EYES POPPED open in the murky, early morning light that invaded the dark cabin. Something had woken him. A noise – some kind of thumping noise. Over and over again. And it was cold in the living room, like someone had turned off the heat.

Thump. Thump.

Cole sat up quickly, his fingers already wrapped around his gun, a black H&K nine millimeter with hollow-point bullets. He looked right at the front door – the source of the noise. The door was opening and closing slightly, the door thumping shut, then creaking open a little from the freezing wind outside.

Creak. Thump.

Cole had slept on the floor, blankets spread out around him. He was still fully dressed except for his boots and heavy coat, gloves, and hat. He twisted around and looked at the couch. Stella and David stared back at him in the early morning light, their eyes dinner plates of fear that glistened in the semi-darkness. They stared at Cole, and then they looked at the front door as it creaked open again and then thumped shut.

Cole turned towards Trevor who was already sitting up on his blue sleeping bag. Jose sat near him. Both of them looked like they had just woken up, both still a little groggy, but they both had their pistols in their hands. Cole's eyes darted to the blankets spread out all over the floor – Frank's blankets. But Frank wasn't there.

Everything seemed to be moving in a syrupy slow-motion for

Cole; he was tired, he was sure of that, but this was a degree of grogginess he'd never felt before, like he imagined it would feel to be coming awake from anesthesia after a surgery. He forced his sluggish mind to think. He looked back at Jose and Trevor. "Where's Frank?" he whispered.

"That's what we want to know," Jose whispered back.

Cole sighed, his mind finally chugging back into action, not quite at full steam yet, but getting there. "Who took the next watch?" he asked. "After Frank."

"Not me," Jose answered.

"Me either," Trevor said.

Needles, Cole wondered as he got up and stared at the front door that had just thumped closed again. No, Cole thought. Frank wouldn't have woken Needles up for a watch, not in the mental condition Needles was in these days.

"Who opened the door?" Cole asked.

"It was like that when we woke up," Jose answered.

Cole walked to the front door in his thick socks, his gun still clenched in his hand. A knot of fear wormed its way around his insides. Something was wrong here.

He stood in front of the solid wood door and watched it for a moment. Then he brought his pistol up, ready to aim it at whatever might be outside. He could hear Jose and Trevor getting to their feet. Cole pulled the door all the way open. He stared out at the front porch which was empty – nobody there. Cole relaxed a little, lowering his weapon.

"Is he out there?" Jose asked from behind Cole.

"I don't see him," Cole said. He stepped through the doorway and looked out past the front porch to the front field which was hidden under a blanket of pristine white snow. The line of dark trees stood in the distance like a wall. The snowstorm had stopped sometime during the night and everything was quiet and calm. The scene outside could be the front of a post card, Cole thought. The freezing wind bit at the skin of his face and hands almost immediately, and his feet were turning into ice blocks. "Frank!" Cole called out. "You out here?!"

No answer.

"Frank!" Cole took a tentative step onto the floorboards of the porch. Something in the snow caught his eye, something just beyond the four steps that led down from the porch into the snow. He stared for a long moment.

Cole hurried back inside. He shut and locked the door. He saw that Trevor and Jose were still standing on their blankets and sleeping bags, their guns ready, but they weren't making a move towards the front door. Needles struggled to come fully awake on the recliner; he knuckled sleep from his eyes.

"Maybe Frank's in the bathroom," Cole said as he stood in front of the door, almost like he was blocking it.

"I don't think so," Trevor said. "But I'll check." Trevor took off for the bathroom. They could hear him stomping around in the hall, and then in the bathroom.

Cole's mind was still a little sluggish. He had slept like a rock even though he didn't think he was going to be able to sleep at all, especially with the corpse of the former homeowner stuffed down inside the kitchen freezer. Yet he had slept deeply and without any dreams that he could remember.

Trevor came back into the living room, shaking his head. "He's not back there anywhere. Back door's still locked."

"Where the hell would he go?" Cole asked as he hurried over to Frank's blankets. He rummaged through the blankets and sheets. He found Frank's coat balled up in the blankets. "His coat's still here," Cole said, holding it up. "His gloves. His hat. He wouldn't have gone outside without his coat and hat."

"What about his gun?" Jose asked.

Cole moved the blankets and sheets around; he tossed the pillow across the room. "I don't see it anywhere."

Jose let out a frustrated sigh.

"Oh shit!" Trevor yelled, startling all of them. Trevor sprang into action; he rushed across the room to the fireplace hearth. He grabbed one of the metal cases, laid it on its side, popped the latch, looked down inside and breathed out a sigh of relief. "Looks like it's all still here."

"You thought Frank ran off with the money?" Jose asked in a disgusted voice.

"Yeah, it crossed my mind."

"Frank would never do that," Jose growled.

"Well, I wanted to rule it out. Is that all right with you?"

"Okay, guys," Cole interrupted. "Let's stay calm and think about this."

Needles, fully awake now, looked around at them. He had stripped down to only his thermal underwear at some point in the night, the small crucifix hung outside of his shirt. The sleeves of his thermal shirt were pulled up to his elbows, revealing even more tattoos covering his thin, sinewy arms. "What happened?" he asked.

"We just woke up," Trevor told Needles. "Frank's not here."

"What do you mean, Frank's not here? Where is he?"

"We don't know."

Cole grabbed his boots and walked to the dining room table. He pulled a chair out, the chair's legs scraped at the floor. He plopped down and put his boots on, lacing them up. He had seen something when he'd opened the front door all the way. At first he wasn't sure if he'd really seen it, but he was pretty sure he had.

"Where are you going?" Trevor asked Cole.

"Outside to look for Frank." He looked at the others. "Alone," he said.

CHAPTER TWELVE

COLE STOOD AT the edge of the porch, at the edge of the steps that disappeared down into the snow. And there they were, just what he'd thought he'd seen when he'd opened the door earlier.

Footprints.

There was a set of footprints in the snow that led from the front porch steps out towards the line of dark trees in the distance. Cole stared down at the footprints, trying to understand why Frank would walk out of the cabin in the middle of the night to the woods. Did he see something out here? Hear something?

Cole pulled his nine millimeter out of his coat pocket. He always wore thin leather gloves on bank jobs, they allowed him to grip his pistol better; they were almost like a second skin covering his own hands. His hands were cold now, but he sacrificed the cold for the increased sensitivity and mobility in his hands. His index finger caressed the trigger lightly as he stared out at the line of trees. There was a ribbon of deep blue sky right above the trees where the sky was beginning to lighten up with the sunrise. But there was also a mass of dark clouds building up in the sky in the other direction, the next storm in this series of snowstorms; right now they were in the calm of the storm, like an eye of a hurricane, a moment of peace and calm.

His boots crunched in the snow as he stepped down into it. He stood in the snow for a moment, which came up to his mid-calf. He stared down at the set of footprints. A man's footprints. Regular gait. Not like this man was running. Like he was walking; a leisurely midnight stroll through the freezing snow to the dark woods.

Cole followed the footprints, staying three feet away from the footprints, careful not to disturb them. His eyes darted around as he followed the trail of footprints to the trees; there didn't seem to be anything threatening out here that he could see, but a hard knot of fear sat in his stomach like a stone.

*

Inside the cabin, Stella got up and walked towards the kitchen.

Jose watched her in shock. "Hey, lady! What the hell do you think you're doing?"

Stella stopped, she looked right at Jose, but she showed no fear of him. "David needs something to eat."

"Did we say you could just get up and walk around?" Jose spat out.

"I didn't ask," she said.

Jose was about to explode with rage, but Trevor's words grabbed his attention. "Leave her alone, Jose."

"What?" Jose said, turning on Trevor now.

"I said leave her alone. She's not our prisoner."

"You aint my boss."

Stella ignored the two men and continued to the kitchen. She wasn't going to wait around for them to quit arguing with each other – that might take forever. She looked through the cabinets.

Trevor turned his attention away from Jose and he watched Stella. "What are you making him for breakfast?"

Stella didn't look at Trevor as she spoke to him. "There are some packets of oatmeal up here."

"How about some coffee for us?"

Now Stella looked right at Trevor who was giving her his sweetest smile, she was sure it worked on most of the ladies. "Sure," she finally answered in a sarcastically sweet voice. "Coffee coming right up."

She pulled out some instant coffee from the cabinet along with the packets of oatmeal.

Oatmeal would be good for her and David, Stella thought to herself as she boiled water on the stove for the oatmeal and started the coffee maker. They were going to need all of their strength for what was coming soon.

*

Outside, Cole followed the footprints. He was almost to the woods now. He glanced back at the cabin, which was at least fifty yards away. He looked back down at the footprints and followed them for a few more feet – then he stopped dead in his tracks.

He stared down at the snow in disbelief, having trouble believing what he was seeing.

A crackling noise deep in the woods startled him. He brought his pistol up and aimed it into the dark woods, his hand shaking slightly, his breath pluming up in front of his face from his heavy breathing.

Nothing moving in the trees that he could see.

He turned and ran back to the cabin. Even in his panic, he made sure that he stayed well away from the set of footprints in the snow. He didn't want to disturb them at all – he wanted the others to see what he had just seen.

*

The oatmeal was ready. Stella poured some in a bowl for David. She looked at David on the couch. "David, I made you some oatmeal."

David stared at her, but he made no move to get up. His long hair was a little rumpled from a night's sleep.

"Come on, David," she said. "You need to eat something."

Trevor got up from his sleeping bag and came to the dining room table. He looked down at the bowls of oatmeal sitting on the table. He looked at Stella with a half-smile on his face. "What kind of oatmeal is it?"

"Apples and cinnamon."

"My favorite."

Stella looked past Trevor at David who still wasn't moving.

Trevor sat down and took a big bite of his oatmeal. "How's that coffee coming?" he asked around a mouthful of oatmeal.

Stella sighed, but she poured cups of coffee and set them on the dining room table. Trevor took a sip. "Perfect," he said.

Jose sat on his blankets and laced his boots up. "I can't believe you're eating that," he told Trevor. "How do you know she didn't poison that stuff?"

Trevor stopped eating suddenly, his mouth hung open as he made choking noises, his eyes bulging. He dropped the spoon back into the bowl and grabbed at his throat, clawing at it, some of the oatmeal dribbling out of the corner of his mouth.

Jose stood up and shook his head. "You're really an asshole, you know that?"

Trevor erupted in a fit of laughter.

Even David cracked a smile.

Stella smiled, too. Her eyes met David's eyes for a moment and she grabbed a bowl of oatmeal for David and brought it to him.

Needles didn't look at anyone or join in the conversation. He sat curled up in the recliner, rubbing his crucifix with his fingers and staring at the front door.

Jose grabbed his coat and slipped it on. He fished his gloves and hat out of the pockets of the coat.

"Where are you going?" Trevor asked around another mouthful of food.

"Going to help Cole look for Frank."

"Who said you could do that?"

"I never asked for permission, did I?"

"He said he wanted to go alone," Trevor reminded him.

"I don't give a shit. Just because Frank isn't here right now doesn't make you and your brother the boss."

Jose turned away from Trevor and took a few steps towards the front door, but then he stopped as the door flew open and Cole rushed inside.

Cole slammed the door shut and twisted the deadbolt lock. He backed away from the door, and then he turned and looked at the others with wide eyes of shock.

"What's wrong?" Jose asked. "You find Frank?"

"He's gone," Cole said in a hoarse voice.

"Yeah, no shit," Jose said. "We can see that."

"No, I mean he's … just gone."

CHAPTER THIRTEEN

THEY ALL FOLLOWED Cole through the snow, all of them bundled up in their coats, hats, and gloves. Cole stopped when they got close to the trees. He pointed down at the snow.

They gathered around, all of them careful to stay away from the set of footprints in the snow. The footprints led from the cabin almost to the woods. About twenty feet before the woods, the footprints stopped, like the person took a step, and then he was gone.

"I don't understand," Jose said as he scratched at his head underneath his knit cap. He looked around. "It's like something picked him up right off the snow."

No one said anything.

Jose looked at the line of dark trees looming in front of them, the unending forest beyond the first line of trees. "This doesn't make any sense," he continued.

Stella and David stood away from the group of men, closer to the trees. David stood in front of Stella, and Stella's hands were on his shoulders. David pulled away from her and walked towards the trees, staring at them with a fierce intensity.

"Honey," Stella said as David took another step through the snow towards the trees. David didn't turn around at the sound of her voice.

"What's wrong with him?" Jose asked.

Needles watched David. "It's like that kid can see something in the woods."

Needles hurried through the snow towards David, a sudden rage on Needles' face. "That kid can see something in the woods!"

Stella jumped in between David and Needles, an animal-like look of protectiveness on her face. "You stay away from him," she growled.

Needles stopped, but he wasn't letting it go. "What's wrong with that kid? What's he see in those woods?"

Cole stepped over to Needles; Cole's hands hung at his sides like a gunfighter's hands, ready to grab at his gun in a flash if he needed to. "Needles, back away from that kid."

Needles looked around, nodding his head quickly. "There's something wrong with those two. I don't know why you guys can't see that."

Cole ignored the babble from Needles as he trudged through the snow and stood beside David and looked at the woods, trying to see what David was seeing. He looked down at David. "You see something in there, kid?"

David looked up at Cole and stared at him with his large dark eyes. He didn't nod yes or shake his head no. He didn't say anything; he just walked back to Stella and grabbed her hand again.

Stella just shrugged.

Cole looked up at the sky. Darker clouds were moving in fast, promising a lot more snow. "Let's get back inside."

*

The men sat around the dining room table, all of them sipping cups of coffee. Stella sat beside David on the couch. David had eaten half his bowl of oatmeal, but then he didn't want any more.

Cole looked at the other men at the table. "I want to know what made Frank get up in the middle of the night and leave."

"You think those are his footprints?" Trevor asked.

"Who else's would they be?" Cole asked.

Trevor shrugged. "I don't know. Maybe he heard something

in the middle of the night. Or he saw something. He went out there to check it out."

"He would've woken us up," Cole said.

"Then maybe he ran," Trevor answered.

All eyes were on Trevor. For a moment a tense silence blanketed the room.

"Frank wouldn't run out on us," Jose growled.

"Hey, I'm just exploring possibilities," Trevor said. "Besides, this is a different situation we're in now." Trevor's eyes rested on Needles. "We've never had a murder rap hanging over our heads before."

Needles stared at Trevor, but he didn't say anything.

"Even with a murder rap," Jose said, "Frank wouldn't run." Jose stared right at Trevor. "But I have a theory – maybe somebody did something to Frank in the middle of the night." Jose's eyes were still locked on Trevor. "Somebody with a lot to gain."

Trevor stared right back at Jose. "You trying to say something, Jose? Go ahead and spit it out."

"Come on, you two," Cole said. "Let's think about this for a minute. Frank leaves in the middle of the night without his hat or coat."

"Or his share of the money," Jose offered.

"Or his share of the money," Cole repeated. "Then he walks straight from the cabin to the woods. And then his footprints just stop."

"Maybe somebody else got him," Trevor said. "He heard something, went out there to check it out and someone got him."

"Have to be a bad motherfucker to take Frank," Jose stared at Trevor.

"You mean like the bad motherfucker that tore a guy's eyes out and stuffed him in a freezer?" Trevor answered.

Cole leaned back in his chair and ran his hands through his hair as he exhaled a deep breath. "This shit doesn't make any sense. There's no sign of struggle anywhere. If somebody got to

Frank, we would've heard something. Frank yelling. Gunshots. Something."

"I slept like a rock," Trevor told them.

"Me too," Cole added. "It was like I passed out."

Needles chuckled. They all looked at him. Needles sat back in his chair, the wood creaking. He laughed harder now. "Nobody's going to say it, are they?" he said through his laughter.

"Needles …" Cole started.

"No, Cole," Needles snapped, his laughter cut off suddenly. His eyes blazed with fear and insanity. "People just don't go out in the middle of the night and walk into the woods. People don't just disappear in mid-step. Something's wrong here. Really wrong."

They were all quiet for a moment. Needles took a deep breath, like he was trying to control himself and he continued. "Something took Frank. Not someone, it was some-*thing*."

"Needles, don't start with that shit again," Cole warned.

"You guys know it's the truth," Needles said, almost under his breath. "You're going to realize it before long."

Cole got up and took his coffee cup to the kitchen. He poured another cup of coffee, spooned a few teaspoons of sugar into it and stirred it – the sounds were loud in the quiet cabin.

Trevor glanced at Needles, at Stella and David, then back at Cole. "Cole, maybe Needles is right."

Cole turned and stared at Trevor. "There's got to be some kind of rational explanation here," Cole told him.

"I'm not seeing any rational explanations." Trevor glanced around at the others for a moment, and then he looked back at Cole. "Maybe it's time we thought about getting out of here."

"I think we should look for Frank," Jose spat out.

"Frank's gone!" Trevor shouted. "He ran. When are you going to get that through your head?!"

Trevor and Jose jumped to their feet; their chairs tipped backwards and fell over on the hardwood floor. They glared at each other, ready to fight. Cole rushed back into the dining room and stepped in between them. "That's enough," he said as he stared at each of them. "We're not going to fight each other."

Neither of them said a word as they grabbed their chairs and sat back down. Cole went back to the kitchen counter for his cup of coffee. He took a sip as he walked back into the living room. He stared at Stella and David. "What about you?" he asked Stella. "Did you hear anything last night?"

"No," Stella answered in a low voice.

Something about her, Cole thought. She's hiding something. He saw her eyes dart to the fireplace, at the cases of money, and then she looked at him again.

"What?" he asked her. "If you saw something or heard something, you'd better spit it out."

Stella hesitated, and then finally she said: "None of you noticed that the ax from the fireplace is gone?"

CHAPTER FOURTEEN

THEY ALL STARED at the fireplace.

Cole remembered now that there had been an ax leaning next to the small stack of firewood set on the hearth. He had thought it was odd that someone would have an ax inside the house, but it looked like Tom Gordon had used it to break up the logs into smaller pieces before placing them into the fireplace.

And now the ax was gone.

"What the hell?" Jose whispered.

Nobody answered Jose. They all stared at the fireplace.

"This just keeps getting weirder," Trevor mumbled.

Cole looked at Stella and David for a moment, and then he looked at the others. "Okay, I'll go check out her truck; see if it can be fixed." He looked at Jose. "You come out there with me. Watch my back."

Trevor jumped to his feet. "You don't want me to come with you?"

"No. You stay here and watch these two." Cole pointed at Stella and David.

Cole walked to the kitchen counter and above the end of the counter on the wall was a wooden key holder carved into the shape of a large key. But there were no keys on the key holder. Cole's eyes scanned the counter where someone might throw a set of keys – but there were no keys on the counter. He opened the first drawer, a junk drawer, and rummaged through it.

"What are you looking for?" Jose asked as he shrugged into his winter coat.

"Probably the keys to Tom Gordon's truck, genius," Trevor said to Jose.

"What the hell's your problem?" Jose said as he took a step towards Trevor.

"Nothing," Trevor said with a smirk.

Cole found a set of keys, but they couldn't be the keys to the pickup truck outside, but they did look familiar and he was pretty sure that he knew what these set of keys went to. He palmed the small set of keys inside his hand and continued his search through the drawers for the keys to the pickup truck.

Then a morbid thought occurred to Cole. What if the keys to the pickup were still in Tom Gordon's pants pocket when he was murdered? What if they were in his pants right now, frozen in there? Cole could imagine pulling the semi-frozen corpse out of the freezer, prying the pockets open or cutting them away with a knife as frozen flesh peeled away with the cloth. He pushed the thoughts away, and moved to the next drawer, opened it and found the truck keys. He closed his hand around the truck keys, collecting them with the small set of keys already in his hand, and he pocketed them both. He turned and looked at Jose. "Found them. Let's go."

*

Cole and Jose walked around the cabin to the back where Stella's Chevy Suburban was parked under a blanket of snow. Jose trudged through the snow right beside Cole, his gloved hands stuffed into his coat pockets. "I don't know what your brother's problem is," he grumbled.

"He's just nervous and trying not to show it," Cole answered. "The more nervous he gets, the more sarcastic he gets."

"He better stop fucking with me," Jose said. "That's all I'm saying."

Cole opened the driver's door and looked at Jose. "You two are going to cool it right now; we have enough to worry about without you two at each other's throats."

Jose looked away and exhaled a long breath that plumed up in front of his face in the freezing air. "Whatever," he mumbled.

Cole still stared at Jose. "Maybe Trevor's right. Something's not right here in this cabin and Needles is halfway to La La land right now and pretty much useless. So the rest of us need to keep our cool and work together."

Jose shrugged his shoulders and kept looking around.

"Jose, I'm serious. I need your help. And Trevor's."

Jose looked back at Cole. "Just get that fucking truck fixed so we can get the fuck out of here."

Cole pulled the latch to pop the hood. He marched through the snow to the front of the truck. He lifted up the hood and stared down at the mess that used to be engine.

Jose saw the look on Cole's face. He hurried over to the front of the truck and stared down at the destroyed engine. He didn't know near as much about engines as Cole did, but he knew enough to know that this engine was ruined. Inoperable.

Cole stuck his hand down in the motor and picked up some loose parts, then he tossed them back down onto the engine, the clanking sound was loud out here in the silence. Cole picked up the cables that used to go to the battery. "Battery's gone," Cole mumbled.

"Holy shit, Cole," Jose yelled right beside him as he stared in shock down at the engine. "Holy fuck, man. What the fuck?"

Cole studied the frayed end of the battery cable. It looked ripped, torn apart, like someone had torn the battery out of the truck with tremendous force, snapping the battery cables.

"What the fuck?" Jose said again as he backed away from the truck, pacing around in the snow in a small circle, still cussing. "What the fuck happened?"

"It looks like someone destroyed the engine with an ax," Cole said, his voice even and controlled, like a scientist analyzing a piece of data. "See those chop marks there. Hell of a swing."

Jose swung his fists at the air. "Fuck!" he screamed out into the freezing air. "FUCK!!" His voice echoed across the snowy field.

Cole lowered the hood of Stella's truck, but he didn't close it all the way. He turned to Jose. "Let's go check the other truck."

*

Inside the cabin, Stella stood at the sink and washed the leftover oatmeal out of the bowls.

Trevor watched her. He still sat at the dining room table, his coffee cup in front of him. He toyed with the cup, spinning it around slowly on the table as he glanced at David who sat on the couch. Needles was curled up in the recliner, comforting himself by rubbing his cross around his neck, his eyes half-closed, his lips moving in silent prayers. Trevor looked back at Stella, watching her rinse the dishes. "What's wrong with your kid?" he asked. "Is he autistic?"

"No," Stella answered, not bothering to look at him.

"Retarded?"

Stella gave Trevor a hard look with her blue eyes. "No," she said.

"Seems like something's wrong with him."

"He just doesn't talk much," Stella said as she turned her attention back to the dishes, setting them in the strainer a little too hard.

Trevor smiled as he kept playing with his coffee cup. "Stella, could I get another cup of coffee? It was really good."

"Get it yourself," she told him without looking at him.

David got up from the couch and walked across the area rug in the middle of the living room; he gave Needles a wide berth as he hurried over to Stella.

Stella turned and smiled at David. "What is it, honey?"

He tugged on her sleeve. She bent down and he cupped a hand beside his mouth and whispered into her ear.

She nodded. "Sure," she said. She went right to one of the drawers in the cabinets and rummaged through them.

Trevor watched the two of them with that same smirk on his face. "What's the kid want?" he asked.

Stella found a spiral-bound book of notebook paper. She handed the notebook to David. His face lit up as he took it. She continued looking through the drawers for something else.

"Is he writing a book?" Trevor asked.

"He wants something to draw on," Stella said over her shoulder as she continued looking through the drawer.

"Really?" Trevor's face lit up. He looked at David. "Are you a good artist?"

David stared at Trevor for a moment, and then he looked at Stella with hope in his eyes.

Stella turned to David with a ballpoint pen in her hand. "Sorry, honey. This is all I could find."

David took the pen with a big smile and he hurried back to the couch, his long hair flying out behind him as he ran. He plopped down on the couch and opened the notebook.

Trevor got up and grabbed his coffee cup from the table. He walked to the coffee pot and poured another cup of coffee. He watched Stella as she went back to the couch and sat down beside David.

Stella looked at Trevor. "You don't seem particularly worried about what's going on here."

Trevor sipped his coffee as he mulled over an answer. "I'm not afraid of anything," he finally said.

You will be, Stella thought.

*

"Pop the hood," Cole told Jose.

Jose lifted the handle on the driver's door of Tom Gordon's truck, and then wrenched the door open as snow fell in heaps from the top of the door and the roof. He reached inside the murky truck – all of the windows covered with snow made the interior dark. He groped around until he found a lever; he pulled until he heard the clunking sound that released the hood.

Cole lifted up the hood. He was pretty sure what to expect, but he still hoped anyway. He prayed that he was wrong.

But he wasn't.

Jose rushed around to the front of the truck, slipping in the snow a little. But then he stopped in his tracks when he saw the expression on Cole's face. "Fuck," Jose breathed out.

Cole slammed the hood of the truck shut. "Somebody doesn't want us to leave," he said.

CHAPTER FIFTEEN

"THERE'S NO WAY you can fix the truck?" Jose asked Cole.

"I don't think so," Cole said as he looked at the large, free-standing garage behind Tom Gordon's pickup truck. "I'm going to check in there. You stay out here by the truck and watch for anything."

Jose nodded, his gun in his gloved hand already. He looked at the woods as Cole stomped through the snow drifts to the double doors of the garage.

Cole pushed on one of the wooden doors. At first it didn't budge, and he thought he was going to have to call Jose to help him, but then it broke free. He slid it open far enough so that he could slip inside. He stood there for a moment in the doorway, breathing hard from pushing the door open, his breath clouding up in front of his face.

Cole entered the garage which was longer than it was wide. On both sides of the garage boxes, crates, and bags were stacked up. There were stacks of lumber and wood siding, cinder blocks, and an old water heater. Cole walked down a pathway through the stacks of junk. He paused and looked at a long workbench stacked with automotive parts. Tools hung from a pegboard above the bench. Boxes were crammed underneath the bench, some of the boxes split open from the weather. Cole wondered if there might be some spare parts to the trucks among the parts on the counter, but it didn't matter – he knew both engines were too far gone to repair in a day or two.

Besides, he was looking for something else in here. His hand went to his pocket, his gloved fingers reached into his pocket and pulled out the set of keys he'd found in the kitchen drawer.

He ventured farther down the aisle through the stacks of junk. He saw boxes and crates stacked on top of each other. A large shelf had been built above the boxes, bags of rock salt stacked on top of the shelf. He saw a red plastic container of gasoline. He walked over to the gas container, lifted it up, about half full. A little farther down a tarp covered something large.

That might be what he was looking for.

Cole pulled the tarp away which was nearly frozen solid, but it broke free, crinkling loudly in the silence. And under the tarp was what he suspected the keys went to. A snowmobile. An older one, but it looked like it might still run.

"Cole!"

Cole turned to the doorway of the garage, towards the sound of Jose's panicked voice. "Cole, get out here right now!"

He threw the tarp back over the snowmobile, covering it completely, then at the last second he pushed some of the boxes down on top of it – he didn't want Jose or Needles discovering it. Then he broke into a run towards the garage doorway and pulled his gun out of his coat pocket.

*

"So, you're an archeologist, huh?" Trevor asked as he stood in front of the coffee maker. He added more sugar and cream to his coffee.

"Yep," Stella answered. She was already getting very tired of whatever game Trevor was trying to play here. She glanced at Needles who was still curled up in the recliner, rubbing his crucifix; he stared down at the large area rug, seemingly transfixed by the colorful patterns. Stella looked back at Trevor. She decided to flip the questions around. "What about you?" she asked. "You look more like a grad student than a bank robber."

Trevor smiled. "Things aren't always what they appear to be."

"Believe me, I know."

"What does a grad student look like?" Trevor asked, and then he sipped his coffee. "You some kind of expert?"

"I've been to college before. Archeology, remember? You need to go to college for that." She wasn't going to let him weasel his way out of an explanation. If anything, it would keep him from asking her more questions. "What made you decide to rob banks?"

"Long story," he told her.

Stella looked around. "Looks like we've got nothing but time right now."

*

Cole ran out of the garage, his gun in his hand. He stopped and looked around for Jose. But Jose wasn't around anywhere. Cole looked at the pickup truck – Jose wasn't there.

A movement in the snow beyond the front of the truck caught Cole's eye – it was Jose, he was running for the woods, almost to the woods now.

"Jose!" Cole yelled.

But Jose didn't stop; he kept on running through the snow, his boots kicking up snow behind him.

Cole ran after Jose. "Jose, wait!" But Jose wasn't stopping. Cole could see that Jose had his gun out, chasing something. Cole ran across the field towards the trees, his leg muscles began to burn from the slight incline of the field. He caught up to Jose twenty feet inside the woods, the trees already closer together here just this far into woods. Jose stood by a tree, his shoulder against it like he was using it as a shield, his gun was out and pointed at the ground, his eyes wild, darting around like he was trying to look everywhere at once. Mucus ran out of Jose's nose down into his mustache – Cole was pretty sure Jose didn't realize this.

Cole took a second to catch his breath. His chest heaved from his sprint across the field, his breath clouded up in front of his face. He looked around at the trees all around them, his pistol ready, his finger on the trigger. Some of the tree trunks were powdered with snow from drifts of snow piled up on them. The trees seemed to go on forever, blending together into a gray darkness deeper into the woods.

"What is it?" Cole breathed out.

Jose didn't answer. He just looked around with his wild-man eyes. His gun hand trembled as he aimed his weapon into the trees.

"Jose?"

Jose finally looked at Cole.

"What is it?" Cole asked. "What did you see?"

"I saw Frank."

CHAPTER SIXTEEN

TREVOR SET HIS coffee cup down on the counter and looked at the cabin door. He looked back at Stella and David who stared at the cabin door. Even Needles tore his attention away from whatever daydream his damaged mind was stumbling around inside of and looked at the door.

"You hear that?" Trevor asked Stella.

Stella nodded. Beside her, David stared at the door with his large, dark eyes, his ballpoint pen poised in his hand over his notebook page that he'd been drawing on. Something out there scared David.

"Sounds like someone's yelling out there," Stella said in a low voice.

Trevor crossed the room in a blur of movement. He pulled his gun out of the waistband of his pants and cocked it. He opened the front door and rushed outside.

Stella turned to David. "Stay right here," she told him. She was about to get up, but he clutched on to her hand, his eyes pleaded with her not to go. "I'm just going out on the front porch," she told him. "That's as far as I'm going to go."

David let her hand go. She got up and hurried to the front door. She slipped out through the doorway, and then pulled the door almost all the way closed. David stared at the door for a few seconds, but then he looked at Needles.

Needles wasn't looking at the door anymore – he was looking right at David. "I know what you are," Needles whispered at David.

*

On the front porch Stella stepped to the edge of the steps that descended down into the snow. She watched Trevor jump from the porch down into the snow and run across the field towards the woods, his gun out, ready to shoot if he needed to.

*

In the woods Cole stood in front of Jose. "You saw Frank?"

"Yeah," Jose answered with a shudder. "He was up here in the woods. Watching us." Jose's eyes darted away from Cole to the trees. "Just … watching us."

Cole glanced at the trees. "You're sure it was Frank?"

"Yes, I'm sure," Jose snapped. "He had on that blue flannel shirt he was wearing before. No coat. No hat. It was him."

Cole looked at Jose. "Did Frank say anything? Did he wave at you?"

"No. He just stood in the woods, and he was staring at me. No expression. Nothing."

"Did he have his gun?"

"I don't think so. I didn't see it." Jose wiped at his nose with the sleeve of his jacket. "I don't know."

Cole looked down at the snow all around them. Then he looked at Jose. "You're absolutely sure you saw Frank."

"I know what I saw."

"There aren't any tracks in the snow."

Jose looked down at the snow. His eyes widened in surprise. He shook his head no in disbelief. "He was here. Standing right here in these trees. I'm sure of it." Jose looked at Cole with wide eyes that were now confused and a little frightened. "I saw him. I swear I did."

"Cole!"

Cole turned towards the sound of Trevor's voice.

"What's going on?" Trevor asked as he ran into the woods.

"Nothing," Cole answered. "We're coming back inside." Cole looked at Jose. "Come on, Jose. Let's get back inside."

Trevor stood at the edge of the woods, his gun ready in his hand. He looked around. "What were you guys yelling about out here?"

Cole knew that Trevor wasn't going to let this go. "Jose thought he saw Frank."

Trevor stiffened. "Frank?"

"Yeah. He thought he saw him up here in the woods."

"I saw him," Jose muttered.

Trevor stepped deeper into the woods, joining Cole and Jose. He scanned the trees, the low-hanging branches, and then the blanket of snow on the ground all around them. "But I don't see – "

"I know," Cole finished quickly. "There aren't any tracks in the snow."

"I saw him!" Jose snapped.

"Come on, Jose," Cole said in a calm voice. "Another snowstorm is coming. We need to get back inside the cabin."

Jose lowered his gun and turned back to the field. He walked through the trees to the edge of the field. Cole and Trevor glanced at each other, and then they followed Jose out of the woods. Cole could read his brother's thoughts – Jose is losing it now, just like Needles.

Jose stopped at the edge of the clearing and stared at the cabin which sat in the middle of the field over a hundred yards away. He could see Stella standing on the front porch watching them. Jose wondered why Stella was on the front porch watching them.

She has something to do with all of this, his mind whispered to him.

Jose looked up at the sky which was dark gray with clouds. It looked like a wall of gray snow was heading right for them.

"Come on," Cole urged Jose on. The wind from the coming

storm was already picking up; a wave of even colder and nastier weather was coming, if that was possible. "We need to get back into the cabin. We've got other problems to discuss."

"What other problems?" Trevor asked.

Cole glanced at Trevor, but then he nodded at the snowstorm that was moving in fast. "We need to hurry," he told Trevor.

The three ran across the front field as the whitewash of a blizzard swept across the back field behind the cabin.

By the time they reached the front porch, the snowstorm was right on top of them. They hurried inside the cabin.

CHAPTER SEVENTEEN

"DESTROYED?" TREVOR ASKED, his face slack with shock. "What do you mean, destroyed?"

"The engines in both vehicles are destroyed," Cole told him. He looked at Stella and David but they didn't seem too surprised to hear the news. He looked at Needles who didn't seem so surprised either. He looked back at Trevor. "Like someone took an ax to the motors."

Trevor stared at Cole. His mouth moved, like he was trying to say something, but his voice wasn't working for a moment. He turned and paced into the kitchen. Then he turned back to Cole. "An ax? Like the ax that's missing from the fireplace?"

Cole didn't say anything. He didn't have to.

Cole looked at Stella and David. David had a spiral notebook on his lap and a ballpoint pen in his hand. Cole wondered for a split second where David had gotten the notebook and pen, but then he dismissed the thought. He didn't really care right now. Cole watched David draw something in his notebook for a few moments; David was really concentrating on his drawing, his dark eyes focused like laser beams on the page.

"Is there any way the engines can be fixed?" Trevor asked, breaking Cole's hypnosis. The tone of Trevor's voice didn't sound hopeful.

"No," Cole answered as he walked into the kitchen to fix himself a cup of coffee. He poured the coffee into his mug and then held his hands around the cup for a second, letting the heat warm his hands up.

Outside, the blizzard was over top of the cabin like a smothering blanket. The wind howled around the eaves and battered the log walls.

"So, Frank takes the ax with him in the middle of the night and destroys our vehicles with it," Trevor says.

"Frank wouldn't do that," Jose grumbled.

"You said you saw him out there in the woods," Trevor said.

Needles perked up at this news. "Frank's out there?"

Cole watched Stella when she heard that Jose saw Frank. Something about the way she looked. It was only for a split second, but he saw something in her eyes. A fear. But not a fear of Frank, a fear of something else. She knew something about this, Cole was sure. But what?

"No," Trevor spat out the word towards Needles. "Frank isn't out there."

"I saw him in the woods."

"You saw a figment of your imagination. There were no tracks in the snow. No sign of him anywhere. You're tired and scared and your mind's playing tricks on you."

"Don't call me scared, you motherfucker."

"Come on, you two," Cole said.

"If Frank's out there, then why?" Trevor continued on, ignoring Cole's warning.

"I don't know," Jose said. "Maybe he *is* after the money."

"If he's after the money, then why didn't he just shoot everyone when he left in the middle of the night?" Trevor asked. "He would've had the chance. Why didn't he shoot us in Stella's truck? Or at the side of the road? Or when we first got off the snowmobiles?"

"Maybe there's someone else out there," Jose said. "The same people who killed that guy and stuffed him in the freezer. Maybe Frank went out there and they took him. Maybe it's the same people who are after that bitch and that kid." Jose stared at Stella and David. "I think we need to question them. Get some answers out of them."

"Jose, that's enough," Cole said as he stared at him. "We're not going to interrogate anyone. We're not torturers." Cole glanced at Needles. "We're not murderers."

"Yeah, but she knows something."

"If she's involved with this, then how would Frank know where Stella was going to be in her truck?" Cole asked Jose. "We took a different escape route after Needles killed the old man in the bank. Trevor was the one with the map."

Jose turned to Trevor. "Yeah, Trevor had the map. He knew where we were going."

"Oh, so I'm involved with this now?" Trevor said and couldn't help smiling which only seemed to infuriate Jose even more.

"You and your brother, maybe," Jose looked at Cole. "How do I know?"

"Like Cole said," Trevor went on. "We wouldn't even be here if Needles hadn't shot that old man in the bank. You think Needles is in on it too? You think all of us joined together with Stella and David to create all of this," Trevor spread his hands out at the cabin, "just to trick you out of your share of the money?"

"I don't know what to think anymore," Jose grumbled.

"I didn't have anything to do with this," Needles said. "That old man in the bank grabbed me! I didn't grab him, he grabbed me. And I saw things. I saw this place. And he told me the devil was coming. When are you guys going to see what's really going on here? Something's following those two," Needles glanced at Stella and David on the couch, "and it isn't human; it's the devil and now he's after us."

"Needles," Cole warned, "we've heard enough of your theories."

"I say we just kick those two outside," Needles went on.

"If the devil's after them, then let him have them. We'll be a lot safer."

"We're not kicking anyone outside," Cole said, as the anger seethed through his words. "We're not torturing anyone. We're not killing anyone. And we're not kicking anyone outside in the snow."

The others stared at Cole in silence.

"We just came across a bad place," Cole continued, his eyes burning with anger, his patience completely gone now. "A place where a man was murdered, and whether we want to admit it or not, it's getting to us. Turning us against each other."

There was an awkward silence hanging over them for a moment.

"So what are we going to do now?" Trevor asked. "Sleep with all of our guns pointed at each other?"

"We're going to stay here tonight," Cole said. "We're going to wait until these snowstorms pass us by. And we may have to walk out of here tomorrow if we can't get one of these vehicles to work. We'll have to flag down another vehicle out on the road."

"Four wanted bank robbers with two suitcases of money and two hostages walking down the side of the road," Trevor said. "That sounds like a good idea."

"Trevor," Cole said through clenched teeth. "You're not helping the situation."

Trevor didn't retort – he knew when he had pushed his big brother too far.

"Before we leave," Cole went on after he inhaled a deep breath and exhaled it slowly, hoping the deep breath would help his nerves, hoping that it would help the anger building up inside of him. "I think we need to burn this cabin to the ground. There's a dead body in here and we don't need to leave behind any evidence that we were here."

"What about her truck?" Jose said as he hitched a thumb at Stella.

"We'll burn that too," Cole said.

The others nodded.

"Okay," Cole said. "We'll sleep in watches again tonight."

*

Hours later Stella and David slept on the couch. David had his notebook tucked protectively under his arm.

Jose had tried the TV and radio over and over again, trying to get some kind of station or signal, hoping to get some kind of news about the bank robbery. But none of the stations would come in – nothing but complete static. Finally, Jose gave up. He sipped from the bottle of whiskey, but not too much. He wanted to stay sober and ready for whoever was out there waiting for them in the darkness.

Trevor sat at the table for hours and played hand after hand of solitaire with a deck of playing cards that he'd found.

Needles curled up in his recliner and massaged the crucifix around his neck as he muttered silent prayers with his eyes closed. Soon he drifted off into a fitful sleep.

Cole took the first watch as the rest of them slept. He planned on waiting until three o'clock in the morning and then waking Trevor up. They would need to take turns on watch if they had to stay here one or two more nights – even Needles would have to take a watch.

Cole's thoughts melted together, and his eyes slowly closed, and he drifted off to sleep without even realizing it.

CHAPTER EIGHTEEN

STELLA WOKE UP in the middle of the night and she began to scream.

Cole snapped awake in the pitch black darkness of the cabin. For a split second he forgot where he was. It was like he was coming out of some kind of a dream, except he didn't remember any of it; it was more like he was clawing his way out of a cocoon of darkness. But now he was awake and trapped in a real cocoon of darkness.

Cole felt around in the darkness, his hands groped at his blanket and pillows looking for his gun. Then he remembered that he had stuck his gun in the front of his pants. His fingers felt along the front of his pants and they touched the reassuring feel of the steel of his pistol.

He didn't even remember lying down on his bedroll. He remembered sitting at the dining room table with a cup of coffee. He was going to wake Trevor up for the next watch. Had he woken Trevor up and then went to bed and couldn't remember it? He wasn't sure, and he didn't have time to think about it right now because Stella was still screaming.

Cole remained motionless for a moment, his fingers still touching the handle of his gun.

"Cole!" Trevor called out. "Where are you?"

"I'm here," Cole called back.

"Stella!" Cole yelled. "What happened?"

Stella's screams stopped, and for a split second the cabin was silent; there wasn't even the sound of the snowstorm outside.

"Are you hurt, Stella?" Cole asked her.

Stella didn't answer. Something about her silence in the pitch black darkness scared Cole even more than her screams. It was like she suddenly realized that there was something in there with them and she didn't want to make a sound and give her position away.

"What the hell's wrong with her?" Jose snapped. "Where's everyone else?"

"I'm on my sleeping bag," Trevor called out.

"I'm on my blankets," Cole said.

"What happened to the lights?" Needles asked with a tremor in his voice. "Who turned out the fucking lights?"

"Where are you, Needles?" Cole asked, trying to keep his voice calm as he tried to mentally picture where everyone was in the cabin.

"In the recliner," Needles answered.

That only left Stella and David. "Stella," Cole said. "Where are you? Where's David?"

"David's gone," Stella whispered.

Cole's blood ran cold. "What do you mean?" Cole finally asked even though his words sounded stupid to his own ears. Gone meant gone.

"He's gone," she whispered again and there was a movement in the darkness, a rustling of clothing.

"Who's moving?" Jose called out.

"Nobody shoot!" Cole shouted. "Does everyone understand me? Nobody shoots. We can't see anything."

Someone was on their feet and running across the wooden floor of the cabin. Shoes pounded the wood. So loud in the darkness. Someone was running for the front door.

Cole turned to the door and saw the barest outline of the door, a dark blue line that outlined the door. It took him a second to realize that this meant that the door was open just a crack. But before he could say anything, the door swung open wide and he could make out Stella's silhouette in the doorway.

"He's out there!" Stella yelled. "David's outside!"

"Stella, wait!" Cole yelled at her as he jumped to his feet.

But Stella didn't wait, she ran outside.

Cole ran towards the dark blue rectangle of the doorway and followed Stella out onto the front porch, his gun in his hand already. He didn't have his coat or boots on and the freezing air bit at him right away, sinking through his flesh and into his bones. He looked out at the snowy field in front of the cabin and he saw Stella running through the snow to David.

The recent snowstorm had passed and there were cloudless patches in the night sky that allowed some starlight and moon-light to filter down which cast a bluish light on the snow, and Cole could see the dark shape of Stella running towards David.

David was just standing in the deep snow, his back to the cabin as he stared at the dark woods.

*

Stella ran through the snow. The cold bit at her as the snow saturated her pants legs, but she didn't care. Her only thought was getting to David. He was out here with this ... this thing.

She reached David and she dropped down to one knee next to him and grabbed on to him. Tears spilled from her eyes, but she barely noticed. "David," she said, but his name came out in a strangled sob. "What are you doing out here?"

David didn't answer her. He didn't even look at her for a moment. He just stared at the dark trees in the distance. They looked like a black mass of the purest darkness, only the outlines of the tops of the trees to tell what they were.

"David," Stella said as she touched his arm, trying to make contact with him, trying to bring him out of his trance. "You can't be out here. You know that."

David finally looked at her; his dark eyes reflected the

moonlight back to her. His expression was calm. "He called me out here," he finally told her. "Didn't you hear him?"

"No, I didn't," she told him. "But you can't be out here," she said in a soft voice, her teeth beginning to chatter, her body trembling from the cold. "It's not safe out here."

David took her hand and held it. It was like his way of apologizing.

Stella smiled and held on to his hand as she stood up. She could feel the snow saturating her pants legs even more. "We need to get back inside. Okay?"

"Okay," David answered.

They turned and walked back to the cabin through the snow, hand in hand.

*

Jose, Trevor, and Needles funneled out of the doorway of the cabin and gathered on the porch next to Cole. They all had their guns in their hands, ready to shoot, ready to kill.

Jose looked out at the field where Cole was looking. "What the hell's going on?"

Cole couldn't take his eyes off of Stella and David as they walked back towards the cabin. At some point in the night David had walked outside into the snow. Just like Frank. Did he see something in the woods? Did he hear something?

"What the fuck's going on?" Jose said, his voice getting louder and louder. "What are they doing out here?"

"I don't know," Cole finally answered. "David must've walked outside."

"Why?"

"I don't know," Cole said.

"Something's not right about this," Jose grumbled.

Cole didn't respond.

"You know he's right," Trevor said. "Why would that kid walk out here in the middle of the night?"

Cole watched as Stella and David walked up the steps onto

the porch. They were both shivering, but Stella was shaking more than David even though he'd been outside longer than she had. Cole thought her trembling had more to do with fear than the cold – not only the fear of who was out here, but the fear of losing David. She had never admitted that David was not her son, but it was obvious that she loved him like a mother.

Stella stared at the four men. "You mind moving so I can get him inside?"

Trevor and Needles moved out of the way. Jose hesitated for a moment and then moved aside. Stella and David hurried inside the dark cabin.

Cole turned and followed them inside. Trevor and Needles entered next. Jose took a few more looks around out at the dark night, he didn't see any movement anywhere, didn't hear any sounds. He turned and entered the cabin.

Jose closed and locked the front door of the cabin, plunging the cabin into near pitch black darkness again.

"Trevor," Cole called out. "We need to get some kind of light on in here."

Trevor's Zippo lighter flicked in the darkness. Trevor's face came into view right behind the flickering flame of his lighter; his face was an eerie mask floating in the darkness. He turned to the kitchen and his mask drifted towards the counters. Cole could hear Trevor rummaging around in the drawers and cabinets.

"I can't find a – " Trevor's words were cut off as he found something. "Wait. Here's a candle. And another one."

Trevor lit both of the candles and put them on small plates. They didn't give off a tremendous amount of light, but they pushed the darkness back a little.

Trevor held one of the plates and gave the other one to Needles. Needles seemed a little more relaxed now that he was holding the light.

Jose went into the kitchen and tried a few of the light switches. "So what happened to the fucking power?" Jose finally said.

No one had any answers.

"Those psychos out there cut the power," Jose said as he walked back into the living room.

"No power means no heat," Trevor said. "That's not good."

"Let's not panic yet," Cole told them. "We have a fireplace if we get desperate."

Jose looked at Stella and David who stood a little behind Cole, like he was protecting them. Stella wrapped her blanket around her and David. They had both stopped shivering now. "I want to know what that kid was doing outside," Jose said.

"Leave them alone," Cole said.

"No. I want to know. I'm sure everyone else here wants to know. There are some psychos outside cutting the power and that kid decides he wants to go outside and stand in the snow."

"We don't know that the power was cut," Cole said as he sighed. "We just had a snowstorm. It could've caused a power outage."

"Yeah, maybe, but I don't think so."

"He was just scared," Stella said. "That's all. He was just confused for a moment. He had a bad dream and forgot where he was."

Jose laughed out loud, a sharp and insane sound in the darkness. "Oh, you're trying to say he was sleepwalking? That's bullshit, lady!"

"Jose," Cole said in a warning voice.

"No, wait," Trevor said. "Jose's right for once in his life. There's something weird about that kid being out there. You have to admit that, Cole."

Jose took a step towards Stella and David, but he stared down at David. "What were you doing out there, kid?"

David just stared up at Jose.

Stella moved more in front of David, and their blanket slipped down to the floor. "Leave him alone," she growled at Jose.

"He knows something about all of this," Jose said in a low, menacing voice.

"He's just a kid," Stella said through gritted teeth.

"He knows something about all of this," Jose continued. "And so do you."

"Jose!" Cole snapped.

Jose turned on Cole. "Fuck you, Cole! I want to know what the fuck that kid was doing out there in the middle of the night!"

"He doesn't want to talk," Cole said.

"How come every time we want to question these two, you're always protecting them?" Jose asked Cole.

Cole was about to answer Jose, but David's voice silenced them all.

"He called me out there," David said, his was voice low but clearly heard in the dark cabin.

Cole turned to David. "Who called you out there?" he asked in a gentle voice.

"He's coming tomorrow morning," David answered.

CHAPTER NINETEEN

JOSE WENT BERSERK. He rushed at Stella and David. "What the fuck kind of game is that kid playing?!"

Stella stepped in front of David and protected him with her body, ready to fight to the death to protect him.

Even though Jose was enraged, he stopped right in front of Stella.

"You back off right now," she growled at Jose.

"You gonna make me?"

Cole stepped in and pushed Jose back. "Jose, back away."

"Cole, they know something. They're hiding something."

"Just back up and we can talk about this."

"I'm through talking. They know something about this. They know something about Frank. About whoever trashed the vehicles. About the electric being cut off. And I want some answers!"

"He's right," Needles jumped in. "I think those two are very much involved in all of this."

"Everybody just calm down," Cole. He glanced at Trevor, making sure his younger brother had his back. Things were about to spiral out of control very soon, Cole thought, and he needed Trevor on his side.

"Everybody just calm down," Cole said again. "We've got some things to – " Cole's words were halted as the electricity suddenly came back on.

Every light and appliance was on at the same time. The TV and radio blared static. The microwave oven was on. The coffee maker on the counter sizzled.

They all looked around the cabin, and then they looked at each other.

"Cole," Trevor whispered to him, his voice barely heard above the blaring TV. "We didn't leave all of these lights on. Or the TV."

Cole rushed over to the TV and turned it off. He shut off the small radio. He headed over to the kitchen and shut off the microwave, the blender, and the coffee maker. It was quiet in the cabin now that the noises were shut off. He turned back to the others who were still huddled together in the living room.

"We didn't leave all of this stuff on," Trevor said again to Cole.

Jose looked at David. "He did it. He went outside in the middle of the night. He must've turned all of this shit on before he left."

Stella snorted sarcastically.

"And then what, Jose?" Cole asked. "Then he went outside and cut the power off?"

"Maybe," Jose said. "Who knows what the hell those two are doing?"

"He's a busy kid," Trevor said.

"Fuck you," Jose looked at Trevor. "I know you don't want to believe that the poor innocent kid is involved in all of this, but he is. He just admitted it to you. He just told you that someone called him out there. And that someone is coming tomorrow morning. There are people out there, people either they were running from or people they are helping. And they're doing this to us." Jose looked at Stella. "What kind of game are you guys playing?"

No answer from Stella.

"Because you're not going to win," Jose growled at her, and lifted his gun a little to let her know he meant business.

Jose took another step towards them. Stella took a step back, still standing in front of David. "Who's coming tomorrow, kid?" Jose growled.

David looked frightened of Jose.

"Answer me, you little freak!"

"That's enough!" Cole stepped in front of Jose and pushed him back a step. "I'm not interrogating a fucking kid. Who knows if he's even telling the truth?"

"I guess we'll find out tomorrow morning," Trevor said.

"Yeah, I guess," Cole said.

"Protecting them again," Jose said as he stared at Cole, then he looked at Trevor.

Cole ignored Jose. "If we're going to walk out of here tomorrow, then we need to get some rest. We'll sleep in watches again. I'll take the first watch."

"It doesn't matter who's on watch," Trevor said, "because I'm not sleeping anymore tonight."

"Me either," Jose said. "I'll be up the rest of the night and on watch. I guaran-fucking-tee that."

*

As the murky light of early morning invaded the cabin, Jose and Trevor slept like babies on their bedrolls. Trevor was wrapped up in the blue sleeping bag that he had called dibs on.

Cole sat at the dining room table. He glanced at Jose and Trevor as their words echoed in his mind. I'll be up the rest of the night and on watch. I guaran-fucking-tee that. Cole smirked and sipped his cup of coffee.

A stirring noise from the living room grabbed Cole's attention. He turned and saw Stella walking towards him out of the gloom from the living room. "Is there some more coffee?" she asked as she reached the dining room table.

"In the pot," he told her. "Help yourself."

Stella made a cup of coffee. She was slow about preparing the coffee. She sat down at the dining room table, close to Cole.

Cole looked at Stella with tired eyes. "Who's out there? Who's chasing you?"

Stella didn't answer right away. She took a sip of her coffee. She glanced into the living room to make sure everyone else was still sleeping, and then she looked at Cole. "You wouldn't believe me."

Cole stared at her for a moment. He wasn't angry, his face was expressionless. "You know who's coming this morning, don't you?"

"Yes."

"Are they after the money?"

"No."

"Are they after you and David?"

Stella was about to answer but a noise from the living room startled both of them – the sound of someone unlocking the deadbolt on the front door. Cole was up in a flash, his gun in his hand, ready to shoot.

But they saw David at the front door. David froze when he saw Cole with the gun pointed at him; he stared at Cole. "He's outside waiting for you," David said in a soft voice. "Can't you hear him calling you?"

Cole glanced at Stella. "Get David away from the door."

Stella rushed over to David and pulled him gently away from the door and ushered him back to the couch.

Cole jolted Trevor and Jose awake. They both jumped up, a grunt escaping Jose as his hands searched for his gun. "Whadisit?" Trevor grunted as he tried to shake off the cobwebs of sleep. "I was awake," he lied.

"He's out there," Cole said to them, and then he looked at Jose. "Get Needles up."

Jose kicked the side of the recliner and Needles sat straight up, his eyes suddenly wide open.

"Who's out there?" Jose said as he turned back to Cole.

"The one coming to see us this morning," Cole reminded him. "The one David was talking about."

Cole pulled his thin leather gloves out of his coat pockets and wriggled his hands into them. He put his coat and hat on and checked his gun and racked a bullet into the chamber, ready to fire. He clicked the safety off. "Everyone get your weapons ready."

Trevor and Jose got their coats on and already had their weapons in hand. Needles shrugged slowly into his coat. Stella and David waited on the couch, huddled together. David stared at the front door of the cabin almost like he could see through it.

Cole looked at Trevor and gestured at him to check the front window. Cole crept towards the front door, ready to open it and charge out onto the front porch.

Trevor stood beside the front window and pulled the curtain back a little so he could peek outside, his gun up beside his head, his finger on the trigger.

"What is it?" Jose hissed. He stood on the other side of the door, ready to run out right after Cole to back him up. "How many are out there?"

Trevor stared out the window for a long moment. He didn't seem afraid, more like he was confused about what he was looking at.

"Only one," Trevor answered Jose.

"One?" Cole asked.

Trevor backed away from the window and looked at Cole, shock on his face. "It's Frank," he said.

"Frank?"

"I told you I saw him," Jose said. "You guys didn't fucking believe me. I told you I saw him out in the woods."

"What's he doing out there?" Cole asked Trevor, ignoring Jose.

Trevor shrugged his shoulders. "Nothing. He's just standing

in the snow and staring at the cabin. Like he's waiting for us to come outside."

"Does he have a gun?"

"I didn't see one."

They could hear something from outside. A voice. Someone calling their names. Calling them to come outside.

"This could be a trap. They could be using Frank as some kind of bait. We all have to be ready for that." Cole looked at Stella, hoping for some kind of help, some kind of acknowledgment, but he didn't get any.

Cole took a deep breath and opened the door and stepped out onto the porch. Jose followed, and Trevor was right behind him.

Needles hesitated before going outside. He looked at Stella and David like he knew something about them, like he knew about the secrets they were keeping. "You coming out there?" he asked Stella.

Stella nodded. "Yeah. We need to get our coats."

Needles was willing to wait for them.

Stella and David grabbed their coats from the end of the couch. Stella helped David get his shoes on.

Needles still waited for them.

Stella and David glanced at each other, they were ready. Needles gestured at the door with his pistol. "Let's go," he told them, and he waited for them to go outside first.

They walked to the doorway with Needles right behind them. Stella had a feeling that Needles was going to aim his gun at the back of their heads and pull the trigger and end their lives in an instant. But he didn't. The three of them stepped out onto the front porch, out into the bitter cold air. The floorboards of the front porch creaked and popped under the weight of all of them standing in a tight group on the porch staring out at the front field.

Frank stood in the snow thirty yards away from the cabin. He wore the same clothes that he'd walked away in, the blue flannel shirt and dark pants. He wore no coat, no hat, no gloves. But he seemed unaffected by the cold. He just stood there, the snow up to his calves. He was statue-still and his head was cocked to the side just a bit.

"Frank," Cole called out as his breath misted in front of his face in the freezing air. He clenched his gun in his gloved hand. "Where have you been all this time?"

Frank just stared at them, his body motionless, his eyes lifeless, his face slack, his head still cocked at that strange angle. For a moment Cole didn't even think Frank was going to answer him, but then Frank's face twitched and he smiled. But it was a fake smile, a wide grin that didn't even touch his dark eyes. This person looked exactly like Frank, but he didn't seem like Frank. Frank would've never had this goofy grin on his face, and it made Cole's skin crawl. This wasn't Frank. It couldn't be.

"Frank!" Cole called out again. "Where did you go? Why did you leave in the middle of the night?"

"He called me out here," Frank finally answered, his voice was guttural and deep and not like his own voice. And when he spoke, that strange smile never left his face. "I don't expect any of you to understand."

"Understand what?" Cole yelled out to Frank.

"He wants things, and you have to give him what he wants!"

CHAPTER TWENTY

"YOU HAVE TO give him what he wants!" Frank said again through that strange smile on his face, his head cocked to the side, his body motionless in the snow.

"Or what?" Trevor yelled. Trevor was jumpy, ready to charge out into the snow. His gun hand twitched just a bit. Cole hoped his little brother would hold his cool for a few moments longer. Trevor had always been the more hotheaded of the two brothers, more impulsive.

Frank's lifeless eyes and plastic smile focused on Trevor. "Or bad things will happen, Trevor."

"What kind of bad things?" Trevor asked.

Frank's smile dropped suddenly and his face went slack. Somehow this expression was even scarier than the creepy fake smile. "Things you won't even believe."

"Frank!" Cole yelled. "Who called you out here? Who are you working with?"

Frank didn't answer.

"This is bullshit," Trevor whispered to Cole through clenched teeth. "Let's just rush out there and get him. It doesn't look like he has his gun."

"Wait a minute," Cole whispered back, never taking his eyes off of Frank. "Something's not right here." Couldn't Trevor see that? Couldn't he see that this person out in the snow wasn't the Frank that they all knew?

Cole waited for an answer from Frank, but Frank still didn't speak; he just stood in the snow with his head cocked to the side just a bit, his face slack, his expression blank.

Cole tried a different approach. "Frank, are you hurt?"

No answer again from Frank. It was like Frank was thinking this over, his expression and eyes still blank.

"Did you hurt yourself?" Cole asked again.

"I'm hurt," Frank finally answered. "It's pain that you couldn't possibly imagine."

"Come on inside, Frank!" Cole yelled to him. "We can help you."

"Cole," Jose whispered to him. "There's something fucked up about Frank."

Cole glanced at Jose, then at Needles who stood behind Trevor. Cole looked at Stella and David; they both stood closer to the front door of the cabin like they were ready to bolt back inside if they needed to. Stella's eyes met Cole's, but she didn't say anything, she didn't offer anything. He looked back at Frank, waiting for an answer from him.

"I can't come inside right now," Frank answered. "He wants things and you have to give him what he wants."

"Who wants things?"

"You wouldn't understand."

"What does he want?" Cole asked.

"He wants all of the money you took from the bank on the front porch," Frank told them in his strange guttural voice. His speech was slower, like he was concentrating on every word.

Jose took a step forward and raised his gun up.

"Jose," Cole growled.

"The money," Jose hissed. "All of this is about the money."

"You have four hours to put all of the money on the front porch," Frank said.

"What if we don't want to give you the money?" Cole asked Frank.

"Then bad things are going to happen."

"What if we decide to keep the money?" Cole continued. "What if we decide to leave? Just walk out of here."

Frank thought for a second and he cocked his head to the side even more like he was listening to a voice that none of them could hear. Then his face lit up suddenly, like all of his facial muscles were pulled up by invisible strings at once, creating that creepy smile on his face again. "You can't!" he said. "He won't let you leave."

"We'll see about that!" Trevor yelled out to Frank.

Frank's face fell slack again, the smile gone, his expression blank again. These seemed to be the only two expressions Frank had now. "You have four hours to give him what he wants," Frank told them, and then he began to back away from them, backing up towards the woods. But it didn't seem like his feet were moving in the snow. It was almost like he was gliding backwards through the snow towards the trees.

"Cole," Needles said from behind him, his voice trembling just a bit. "What the hell's Frank doing? How the hell is he moving through the snow like that?"

"I don't know," Cole said, never taking his eyes off of Frank.

"Fuck this," Trevor grumbled and charged down the steps into the snow, his gun up and aimed at the retreating Frank. "Fuck you!!"

"No!" Cole yelled. "Trevor, wait ..."

As Trevor squeezed the trigger, a wave of wind and snow kicked up instantly, a sudden blinding blizzard from nowhere. Trevor fired three quick shots into the swirling snow, but the shots were muffled by the snow and wind. Then Trevor brought his arms up to his face, shielding himself as best as he could from the snow that pelted the exposed flesh of his face like hail. Trevor turned and stumbled blindly back up the steps, nearly tripping as he stepped onto the porch, getting under the cover of the roof.

Cole grabbed his little brother and did his best to shield him from the sudden squall of a snowstorm.

The small whirlwind of snow died down as quickly as it had started – it was completely gone now; the world was calm and peaceful again.

They stared out at the field.

Frank was gone.

CHAPTER TWENTY-ONE

"WHERE THE FUCK did he go?" Trevor asked as he stared out at the empty field of snow.

"I don't know," Cole answered.

"I don't see him anywhere," Trevor went on, his voice a little shaky. He wiped at his face which was wet and a little red from where the snow had pelted him moments ago. "Do you guys see him in the trees anywhere?"

"We need to get back inside," Needles said in a trembling voice. His eyes bulged with fear as he stared out at the field of snow. "It's not safe out here."

Stella and David didn't wait for the others. Stella ushered David back inside the doorway.

Needles turned and caught the front door as it began to close. He stared inside at Stella and David. "No way. You're not going inside by yourself and locking us out here." Needles hurried in after them.

Cole thought that he'd better get back inside with them, Needles was becoming more and more unglued every second. "Yeah," he told the others. "Let's get back inside."

They all filed back inside the cabin, Cole was the last one inside. He shut and locked the front door. His mind was whirling, spinning. Everything seemed to be happening too fast. He needed things to slow down so he could think.

Jose paced into the kitchen, his movements quick and jerky, he was edgy and upset. "Fuck, man. Frank's been doing this shit all along. All to get the money." He looked right at Trevor. "I told you I saw Frank out in the woods. And you guys didn't believe me."

Trevor didn't answer Jose, he looked at Cole instead. "So, what are we gonna do now?"

Cole didn't answer.

"What do you mean?" Jose nearly screamed as he rushed back into the living room. "What are we gonna do about *what*?"

"The money," Trevor said slowly like he was talking to an idiot.

"I'm not giving up my share of the money," Jose spat the words out. "I'm not putting it out there."

"I want my share out there," Needles said quickly.

Stella and David took their spot on the couch. David wasted no time in picking up his spiral notebook. He opened it to the middle, to a page he had left off on, and he started drawing again at a furious pace. Stella tried to peek at what David was drawing, but he shielded the page with his hand and his body. She hadn't been able to see what he had been drawing at all. She had asked him a few times to see the drawings, but he didn't want her to. And she didn't push, if this was his way of dealing with their situation right now, then she had to let him have his escape.

Needles looked at Cole, Trevor, and then Jose with frightened eyes. He was scared, more scared than any of them had ever seen him. He nodded his head quickly. "I want my share of the money out there," he repeated.

"You're fucking nuts," Jose said to Needles. "It's just Frank out there. Not the boogeyman or the devil."

"So where did that wall of snow come from when Trevor tried to shoot at Frank?" Needles asked Jose. "You saw that … that thing out there. That wasn't Frank. That was … was something else. You saw the way he was sliding through the snow back to the trees. How was he doing that?"

"Fuck this," Jose grumbled. "I'm not having a conversation with a lunatic."

Cole looked at Trevor. "What about you, Trevor? What do you want to do about the money?"

"I don't know yet," he answered.

"Are all of you crazy?!" Jose shouted.

Cole looked at Jose. "Jose, you need to think about this. There are some strange things happening here. Things that aren't easily explained."

"It's just Frank."

"Why would Frank go through all of this trouble?" Cole asked Jose. "Like Trevor said before, why didn't Frank just take all of the money when he went outside in the middle of the night while we were asleep? Or why didn't he just shoot us?"

"I don't know," Jose snapped at Cole. "I don't know why he's doing this. Or how. Or who else is helping him. I just know that I'm not giving them my share of the money."

Jose took a few steps away, and then he turned back to Cole and Trevor. "Somebody has to be making Frank do this. It's the only thing that makes any sense. Whoever took Frank in the middle of the night sent him back to get the money." Jose looked at Stella. "Whoever she's running from followed her here and realized that we were the bank robbers who had stolen the money from the bank. And now they want it all."

Stella stared at Jose as he walked towards her.

"Who's following you?" Jose demanded from Stella.

David put his pen inside his notebook and closed it. He clutched onto Stella with his notebook in his lap and stared at Jose with wide, unblinking eyes.

"Jose," Cole warned.

Jose turned and stared at Cole. "Why do you keep protecting them?"

"We're not going to go over all of that again, are we?" Cole said. "None of us are involved in this. When are you going to get that through your head?"

"Okay," Jose said, nodding his head quickly. "If that's true, then why don't we do a little test? None of us put our money out there. Call Frank's bluff, or whoever's out there with him. Call their bluff."

The cabin was quiet for a moment.

Cole finally shrugged. "Why not?" Cole looked at Trevor. "What do you think?"

"I don't want to give my money away," Trevor answered. "I worked hard for this."

Needles stood in front of the recliner, his crucifix swinging back and forth slightly from his necklace, his wild hair spiked out in different directions, his eyes bulging. "No, I want my share out there. I'm not messing with the devil."

"It's not the devil," Jose said. "I'm so sick of hearing you say that."

"I get a vote," Needles continued. "And I want my share of the money out there on the porch."

"You get a vote," Cole agreed. "We all get a vote. But this is going to be a majority rule."

Needles looked like he was on the verge of panicking. "Why can't we just split the money up now? We each hold on to our own share. We each do whatever we want with it."

"You know we don't split the money up until we're ready to go our separate ways," Cole said. It was something they had always agreed on. Until they were in a safe place where they could all leave, they didn't split the money up. It was too easy and tempting for one person to take his share and leave. With the money all in one place and with all of their eyes on it, it gave the group safety.

"You're such a pussy," Jose said to Needles.

"Enough, Jose," Cole said. "Let's take a vote. We know what your votes are Jose and Needles." Cole turned to Trevor. "What about you?"

Trevor thought it over for a moment. He looked at the two cases of money on the fireplace hearth, and then he looked back at Cole. "I think someone out there is after this money. They don't want to charge in here and take it so they sent Frank back. I say we call their bluff and see what they do. I say we find a way to get to them, a way to get Frank back."

They were silent for a moment, and then Jose looked at Cole.

"And what about you, Cole?"

Cole sighed. "I agree. We keep the money and find out who's out there."

"There's an easier way of finding out who's out there doing this," Jose said as he rushed towards Stella and David. "Who the fuck's out there?!" Jose screamed at Stella.

Jose pulled his gun out and aimed it at Stella. He stared at her with cold, dark eyes.

Cole crossed the room in a hurry. "What the hell do you think you're doing?"

"Getting some answers from this bitch," Jose said. "Once and for all."

CHAPTER TWENTY-TWO

STELLA STARED UP at Jose as David clung to her; but she didn't flinch. She was afraid, but she couldn't show fear of him, she needed to be strong. David inhaled sharply when Jose jabbed his gun at them; he ducked his head underneath Stella's arm and hid behind her.

Stella knew she needed to be strong for David, but a small voice whispered at her from somewhere in the back of her mind. Maybe it wouldn't be so bad, the voice whispered. Just let him shoot, and it would all be over for her. She wouldn't have to go through this anymore. She wouldn't have to go through this again.

But she knew what would happen to her body even after she was dead.

She sat very still as she stared at the barrel of Jose's gun pointed at her. She had seen things far worse than anything Jose could do to her, so she showed no fear of him. Let him shoot you, that small voice whispered again. And then all of this will be over.

But she had to protect David. She still had him to think about; it was the only thing that kept her going.

"I don't know what's out there," Stella answered Jose. "And that's the truth."

Cole moved closer to Jose, trying to calm him down, talking to him in a soothing voice. "What are you going to do, kill the only person who might know anything about what's going on out there?"

"Not unless she tells me what's going on here," Jose growled.

It was like this before at the dig site, Stella thought. But those people were scientists; they were reasonable – at least they were reasonable in the beginning before things got too bad. But these men in the cabin were bank robbers. They were criminals. And they had murdered at least one person that she knew about; the old man in the bank that they kept talking about. She couldn't risk it much longer. She had to tell them something, but she knew she couldn't tell them everything.

"What do you mean, you don't know *what's* out there?" Jose asked Stella.

"It's not people out there," Stella told Jose.

"I told you," Needles said and jumped to his feet, a strange smile of victory on his face – a lunatic smile. "I told you the devil's out there."

Jose glanced quickly at Needles, and then he looked back at Stella.

"Is that what you're trying to say?" Jose asked her. "The devil's out there? The devil's the one that's following you?"

"I don't know what it is."

Jose was about to explode with anger. Stella could see his finger tightening around the trigger.

"I swear, that's the truth!" Stella yelled at Jose. "Something's out there, but I don't know what it is!"

"Let her talk," Cole said, trying to keep Jose calm. "Let her explain."

"The dig site where we came from," Stella continued quickly. "Something like this happened there. People were taken. One by one. I took David and we managed to get to my truck and get away."

Jose stared at her.

"That's the truth."

Stella could see a movement out of the corner of her eye, Trevor sneaking up behind Jose, but she made herself look back at Jose.

Cole stared at Needles who seemed like he was about to alert Jose about Trevor, but after the look from Cole, Needles slumped back down in the recliner and didn't say anything.

Cole turned and looked at Stella with compassion. He's trying a different approach, she thought.

"Stella, we need your help," Cole said. "Whatever you know about what's going on out there could help us. I wish you would tell us."

"You need my help?" Stella asked sarcastically and she couldn't help the bark of a laugh that came out of her. "You run us off the road, carjack us, bring us to the middle of nowhere in a snowstorm, point guns at our faces, threaten to torture and kill us, and then you want my help?"

Cole sighed.

Stella could see Trevor creeping up right behind Jose, but she wouldn't give him away.

"I'm not helping you," Stella went on, trying to distract Jose from Trevor sneaking up behind him. "Not until you stop pointing your guns at me and threatening us."

Trevor aimed his gun at the back of Jose's head, the barrel touching his head. "She's right," he told Jose. "Lower your gun."

"What the fuck, man?" Jose said, and a nervous laugh escaped him. "You're going to shoot me over this woman?"

"And that kid," Trevor said. "You heard Cole. We're not going to kill anyone else. Especially not a woman and a child."

"But they know something."

"I don't care."

Jose sighed and dropped his gun hand. He shoved his gun into the waistband of his pants, and then he walked away. He shook his head as he stared at Cole and Trevor. "You guys are making a big mistake."

"We're going to wait here for the next four hours and see what happens," Trevor told Jose, his eyes dead on him, his gun still in his hand. "We're going to call their bluff, just like we all agreed."

CHAPTER TWENTY-THREE

FIVE HOURS LATER the afternoon shadows grew longer, stretching across the snow as the sun dipped lower behind the trees.

Inside the cabin, Trevor sat at the dining room table with another hand of solitaire laid out in front of him. His gun was close by, and he was ready to grab it if he needed to.

Everyone was tense as they waited.

Needles looked even more nervous now that their four hours were up. He glanced over at the two metal cases of money on the fireplace hearth like he was ready to grab them and bolt for the door, throw them outside in the hopes that it wasn't too late. But he didn't get out of his recliner. He just looked at the front door, and then he looked back down at the rug on the floor. The rug was colorful, full of patterns that seemed to change shape after a while. The more Needles stared at the colors and patterns, the more they seemed to change and move, morphing into something unworldly.

Jose paced from the living room to the kitchen, then back to the living room again. He couldn't sit still. He looked at Cole who sat at the dining room table with his brother, another cup of coffee in front of Cole.

"What's our plan now?" Jose asked Cole.

"We sit tight for a little bit," Cole answered. "See what they do next."

"It's been longer than four hours," Jose reminded him.

"Frank said we had four hours, and it's been longer than four hours. Nothing's happened. Nobody's coming for us."

Cole sipped his coffee.

"We gotta do something soon," Jose continued. "It's going to be dark in a few hours. Then we'll have to stay another night."

Cole still didn't answer.

"I don't want to stay in this place another night. We should do something. Go out there and look around. Try and find these motherfuckers out there."

Cole glanced at Jose. "Just keep watching out the window."

Jose shook his head and walked into the living room. He gave Stella and David a sneer as he walked over to one of the windows near the front door. He pulled the curtain aside and peeked out the window. "Nothing going on out there," he said more to himself than to anyone else.

Trevor stood up and stretched. "I gotta take a whiz," he let everyone know.

"Check the rooms back there," Cole told him.

"I just checked them an hour ago. All the windows are locked. Back door's locked."

"Check them again."

*

Trevor entered the first bedroom down the hall – the guest bedroom. He walked around the bed to the window. He parted the curtains and peeked outside. Nothing. No sign of Frank or anyone else out there. He checked the window. Still locked. He let the curtains fall back in place.

He left the bedroom and walked down the hall, his boots thumped on the wood floor. He checked the back door. Still locked. He entered Tom Gordon's room and checked the two windows in the bedroom – both still locked. He peeked outside at the snowy field that stretched out in all directions from the cabin. He stared at the line of trees in the distance that surrounded the fields like a wall of woods in every direction. The woods had grown darker with the quickly approaching night, but he could still make out the individual trees, and he still didn't see any movement anywhere outside.

Trevor left Tom Gordon's bedroom and walked across the hall and entered the bathroom. He closed the door and walked to the toilet at the other end of the room, the toilet was just under the small bathroom window on the far wall. He took his gun out from the waistband of his pants and laid it on the toilet tank lid; the gun made a loud clinking sound on the ceramic lid when he set it there. He was about to unzip his pants, but something out of the corner of his eye demanded his attention; there was something moving outside the bathroom window in the snow.

He stared out the window, his body frozen in shock. His muscles all sagged at once, like all of the energy had drained out of his body. His bladder let go and the urine ran down his leg inside of his pants. He wanted to scream, but he didn't seem to have any breath inside of his lungs to do so. He just stared out the window, trying to understand what he saw, trying to understand how this could be possible. His mouth moved as he tried to speak, as he tried to scream. "I … I don't understand …" were the only words he could utter in a whisper.

*

Cole sat at the dining room table, the cup of coffee still right in front of him. He had consumed so much coffee throughout the day that there was no way he was going to be able to sleep tonight; he was going to make sure of it. But he had a feeling that at some time during the night, he was going to drift off to sleep without realizing it. It seemed like no matter how much each one of them tried to stay awake, no matter who was on watch, at some point in the long night, they would all fall asleep. Like we're being *put* to sleep, his mind whispered. But he didn't want to think of where that thought came from. What could put them to sleep whenever it wanted to?

Cole glanced over at Trevor's playing cards spread out all

over the dining room table. Then he looked at Jose who leaned against the kitchen counter, still anxious, still unable to sit still for very long. "Trevor's been in the bathroom for a while," Cole said.

"Maybe he had to take a shit," Jose answered.

Cole looked at Stella who sat beside David on the couch as he drew in his notebook. It seemed like David had already gone through nearly half of the pages in the notebook, drawing at a furious pace. Cole figured it was a way the kid dealt with what was going on. It couldn't be easy on a little kid like that to be held captive in a cabin in the middle of nowhere. And coming from whatever they were running from, from wherever they had been, whatever Stella was hiding from the rest of them, had to have taken a toll on him as well.

Cole's thoughts were interrupted when David jumped to his feet quickly; the notebook fell out of his hands, open to a page on the wood floor at his feet. He stared at the front door like something was frightening him.

*

Stella had nearly dozed off when David jumped to his feet. She tried to take every opportunity to nap when she could so she could try and stay awake at night, or at least sleep as lightly as she could.

But she snapped awake when David stood up. She could hear his rapid breathing even before she looked at him, it sounded like he was having a panic attack, struggling for breath. She had seen this happen to him before at the dig site. He stared at the front door.

Something was outside. It had finally come for them.

"What's wrong with that kid?" Stella heard Needles ask from his chair that he always sat in; the recliner – his talisman of safety that he curled up in, a place where he could rub his crucifix and pray to his God that he would be safe. But Stella didn't think God was going to listen to Needles this time – they were all on their own.

"I don't know," Stella lied as she glanced at Needles. "He's scared of something."

Stella looked at David as he stared at the front door with wide, bulging eyes of fear. His mouth hung open, a little slack, his body frozen with fear.

She was about to hold on to David, try her best to comfort him, but her eyes darted down to the open notebook on the floor that David had been drawing in – she could see the open pages, she could see what he had been drawing. What she saw on the pages stopped her mind in its tracks for a moment. She stared at the drawings a little too long. That couldn't be right, could it? her mind whispered. Those aren't what I think they are, are they?

"Stella!" Cole yelled, snapping her momentary hypnosis.

She looked at Cole. "I don't know what's wrong with him," she said again. She would have to figure out what she'd seen in David's notebook later. She would have to confront David about it eventually, ask him how he knew. But for now she needed to put the brakes on her spinning mind and try to act normal – her and David's survival depended on her not revealing too much; she knew that from experience, she had learned that down at the dig site in New Mexico.

"What's out there, kid?" Needles asked in a quivering voice.

David didn't answer Needles. He stared at the front door. Then David's eyes moved away from the door, scanned past the dining room table, to the hallway that led to the two bedrooms and the bathroom.

And that's when they all heard the noise that came from the bathroom – a loud crashing noise.

CHAPTER TWENTY-FOUR

COLE RAN TO the bathroom door. Jose was right behind him, his gun drawn. Cole pounded on the bathroom door. "Trevor!" he called out. "You okay in there?"

No answer.

"Trevor, answer me! Are you okay?!"

Still no answer.

Cole tried the door handle. It wasn't locked, but it seemed like the door was stuck. "Trevor! Trevor, open the door!"

Trevor wasn't answering them.

Cole looked at Jose who stood next to him, his gun in his hand. "I'm going to break the door down. You get ready to shoot if you have to."

Jose nodded – he was ready.

"But be careful," Cole told Jose. "Let's see what's going on before you start blasting away."

"Yeah, man. I'm not going to shoot you."

"I don't want any accidents," Cole said, then he turned back to face the bathroom door. "Trevor, I'm going to break this door down!"

Cole still heard nothing from inside the bathroom. He backed up a step and slammed his shoulder into the door and it almost caved in immediately. Cole backed up another step, ready to ram it again with his shoulder. He had played high school football, strong safety position, and he knew how to hit with his shoulder. Trevor had played high school ball too, his mind whispered, but he pushed the thought away. He didn't want to think of Trevor in the past tense, but he couldn't help feeling a knot of dread worming its way through his body. He rammed the door again with his shoulder, and this time it flew open and slammed against the wall.

The bathroom was empty. Trevor was gone.

Cole entered the bathroom, looking around in shock. Everything looked the same in the bathroom except for two things: Trevor wasn't there and the bathroom window was wide open and damaged around the edges. Cole walked towards the damaged window, the toilet right underneath the window. The toilet lid was up and Trevor's gun was on the toilet tank lid.

"Look," Jose whispered from behind Cole. "Look at the fucking window."

The freezing air from outside invaded the bathroom through the busted and damaged window.

Cole hurried to the window.

"What the fuck?" Jose said from behind Cole as he followed him to the window. "You think Trevor went out that window?" But it didn't seem possible, he thought. The window was too small for a man to fit through.

Cole didn't answer Jose. He drew his gun and pointed it out the window, looking around as much as he could see. "Trevor!" he called. "You out there?!"

No answer from outside, no sound except the freezing wind.

Cole stuck his head and arm out the window; it was as much of his body as he could comfortably fit. The sleeves of his shirt brushed against the splintered wooden frame and the small bits of jagged glass that were still imbedded in the wood. He aimed his gun around outside, ready to fire if he needed to, and he tried to look everywhere at once. But there were no tracks in the snow; there was no blood in the snow, no splinters of wood or broken glass in the snow that Cole could see. He looked at the trees in the distance; there was no movement in the trees, nothing out here at all except the lonely wilderness.

"Trevor!!"

Trevor did not shout back.

"Cole, look at the window."

Cole pulled himself back inside and studied the splintered wood around the window. The wood was cracked in many places, almost like the wood had been twisted by some unimaginable force, like something too big for the window had been pulled through quickly. But what was more disturbing were what looked like claw marks grooved into the wood at the bottom of the window sill, like fingernails had tried to hold onto the wood. And then Cole found the piece of a human fingernail stuck in the groove of the window sill where the window would have come down if it was still there. It was nearly a whole fingernail with blood and a small piece of flesh stuck to the end of it, like it had snapped off completely from a finger.

Trevor's finger.

Cole's mind buzzed with panic. Trevor was gone. His little brother was gone. Someone had pulled his brother out through the window. And they hadn't heard anything in the living room except the crashing of glass and snapping of wood. No screams from Trevor. No gunshots. Trevor hadn't even gone for his gun; it was still here on the toilet tank lid.

How was this possible?

But Cole didn't care how, he didn't even care why at this moment, the only thing he could think of was going outside and finding his brother. He could feel a rage building up inside of him, a rage he hadn't felt in so long, a rage that could make him kill someone.

Cole grabbed Trevor's gun and shoved it down in the waistband of his pants. He brushed past Jose and ran out of the bathroom.

Jose turned to follow him. "Wait a minute, Cole! Where are you going?" Jose ran after Cole who ran right past the dining room table and straight for the front door.

"Wait for me," Jose said to Cole.

But before Cole and Jose even reached the front door, still half a dozen steps away from it, something pelted the front door from outside. Whatever hit the door sounded solid, but it also gave a wet thump when it hit the door.

Cole stopped in his tracks and stared at the door, his gun still in his hand.

Jose stopped, too. He was only a few steps behind Cole. They waited a split second, but it felt like an eternity until they heard the next sounds – it sounded like dozens of objects pelting the front door all at the same time.

"Oh God, no," Cole whispered, and then he ran for the door. He unlocked the deadbolt with trembling fingers, still trying to hold his gun in his hand.

"Wait a minute, Cole," Jose said from behind him.

But Cole didn't hear Jose. He didn't hear or see anything around him; it had all faded away into a white noise. All he could think about was getting to Trevor before it was too late.

Cole unlocked the small lock on the door handle, twisted the knob and swung the door open and stood in the doorway.

It was too late for Trevor.

CHAPTER TWENTY-FIVE

NEEDLES WOULDN'T STOP screaming. It was an insane scream. It was the screaming from someone whose mind had finally snapped. After seeing what was on the front porch, Needles' grip on sanity was nearly gone.

Jose was still a few steps behind Cole who stood in the doorway staring down at the carnage littering the floorboards of the front porch. His body blocked much of what Jose could see, but he did notice the splatters of blood on the front door of the cabin. He didn't want to see what was out there, he didn't want to make his feet move forward, but he had to – he had to back Cole up. He moved to the side of the doorway, nearly beside Cole, but still a few steps behind him, his gun up and ready to shoot. But his gun hand dropped back down as he lost the strength in his body.

Stella let out a cry from the couch and turned David away from the gore on the porch. But she hadn't been quick enough; she knew David had seen it, even if only for a few seconds. But David let her guide his face away even though they had seen this before, they had seen things like this at the dig site in New Mexico.

Cole stared down in horror at the pieces of Trevor's body scattered on the floorboards of the front porch: pieces of Trevor's arms, pieces of his legs, pieces of his flesh; some of the pieces were the size of small hams or turkeys. Most of the pieces of Trevor's body still had clothing stuck to them, the cloth held in place by the drying blood which was so dark in some places it was almost black. A femur bone was splintered at the end of a chunk of flesh that used to be part of Trevor's thigh; the fabric of the jeans was still wrapped around the skin of the leg. Trevor had been cut apart – no, it looked more like he'd been ripped apart, torn apart.

"No …" that was the only word Cole could utter. He could feel his stomach churning, the last meal and coffee he'd eaten and drank threatening to come back up.

Trevor. His brother. His little brother.

The worst part was Trevor's head. It was right there in the middle of the pieces of his body. The head was upright and the eyes were staring at him; flaps of skin from Trevor's neck were spread out underneath the chin like lily pads. Trevor's mouth hung open in a silent scream. His eyes were wide open, staring at Cole; perhaps those eyes were still seeing their last image on earth – some unimaginable horror that had pulled him out through the bathroom window and torn him to pieces.

"Oh God, Cole," Jose yelled from behind Cole. "Shut the fucking door!"

Cole still stood in front of the doorway. He wanted to look away from these pieces that used to be his brother, but he couldn't seem to tear his eyes away.

Jose moved into action; he could see that Cole wasn't going to move, he was too paralyzed by shock. Jose hurried around Cole and slammed the front door shut, and then he twisted the lock on the door handle and then turned the deadbolt lock.

Cole finally came alive; he stared at Jose with a hatred burning in his eyes. "What the hell do you think you're doing?"

Jose stood his ground. "They're out there. We need to shut the door. Get ready to defend ourselves."

"Trevor … he's out there …"

"We can't do anything for him now! He's gone!"

Cole stared at Jose.

Needles' screams had died down, but now he was whimpering as he cowered in his recliner, staring at the front door like he was waiting for it to suddenly crash open. "I told you, Cole," Needles cried. "I told you it was the devil out there! I told you the devil was coming for us!"

"Shut the fuck up, Needles!" Jose screamed at him.

"I told you when we first got here that we shouldn't go inside this cabin. I told you we couldn't stay here. And now it's too late. Now the devil's here and there's nothing we can do."

Jose stomped across the room, his gun aimed at Needles who cowered back into the recliner even more. "I said, shut the fuck up, or I swear to God I'm going to blow your fucking head off."

The cabin was suddenly quiet.

Stella held onto David, her body was nearly in front of his body, protecting him. She knew what was coming next.

She watched Cole who stared at the front door like he wanted to open it again, like he wanted to see his brother one more time, but he didn't want to see him like that.

Then Cole looked right at her.

And Stella saw the rage in his eyes. He marched across the wood floor, his boots thumped on the wood as his long legs made the trip across the floor in a few strides. He stood in front of her, stared down at her. And she was afraid of him at this moment; afraid he would snap and kill her and David.

"Who's out there?" he growled at her.

"I don't know," Stella told him.

"They killed my brother. If you don't tell me …" Cole began.

"I swear to God I don't know," Stella said quickly, interrupting his words. "That's the truth. I don't know what it is. How many times do I have to tell you?"

Cole stared at her.

"I already told you what I know," Stella continued. "At the dig site in New Mexico, it was like this. Something was taking us one by one. I took David and we managed to get to my truck and get away."

"How come your truck wasn't destroyed there like it was here?"

Stella paused for a moment, and then she answered him. "I don't know."

Jose paced across the living room floor, his gun still in his hand. His eyes flicked to the front door and windows every few seconds. "I told you, Cole. I told you earlier that you were making a big mistake."

Cole tried to tune out Jose's voice.

"We should've questioned her more," Jose went on. "We should've started putting bullets in that kid's knees until she told us everything we wanted to know."

Cole's stomach churned at the thought of shooting a small child in the kneecaps.

"She's just bullshitting with us," Jose continued as he paced. "She's just playing fucking mind games with us. There's no monsters out there. There's no devils. It's just some people out there. And either Frank's working with them or they're making Frank work with them. I don't know. I don't care, but it's just some people out there and it's all about the money."

"That's enough, Jose," Cole said.

Jose stopped pacing. They all watched him as his face scrunched in anger and hurt. "You're still gonna stand by that bitch even after your brother was killed by those people out there, the people that she's protecting?"

Cole turned and marched towards Jose.

Jose tensed his body, ready for a fight, but Cole walked right past him and into the kitchen.

"What are you doing?" Jose asked Cole.

Stella could feel David clinging to her arm; she could feel his quick breaths as he held on to her. He was so scared, and he had a right to be. It took a while before they wanted to kill David down in New Mexico, but here it would be happening much more quickly, she was sure of that.

Cole searched through the bottom cabinets until he found what he was looking for – a box of heavy duty black garbage bags. He turned and saw the expression on Jose's face. "I can't leave my brother out there like that," was all Cole offered for an explanation. Cole searched other drawers and cabinets until he found a bag of rubber dishwashing gloves. He slipped his coat and leather gloves on. Then he slid the rubber gloves on over his leather gloves. The rubber gloves were a loose fit over his hands which might interfere with his fingers when he held his gun, but he had to take that chance. He needed to do this for his brother.

Cole grabbed the box of garbage bags from the counter and walked towards the front door.

"So that's it?" Jose said as he followed Cole to the door. "You're just going to let that bitch and that kid sit there on the couch while those people out there pick us off one by one?"

"I'm not torturing anyone," Cole muttered. "And that's it."

You don't know what you're going to do soon, Stella thought to herself. You'll do things you never thought you were capable of. But she couldn't tell them that. She knew that between these three men, Cole was her best chance of staying alive, the only one who seemed opposed to the idea of either torturing or killing her and David, or just leaving her and David here in the cabin while they ran.

Stella knew what Cole would see next. She wanted to warn him, but she couldn't. She couldn't reveal how much she knew, how much she and David had seen. Not yet anyway. Their lives depended on it.

Cole was about to grab the door handle and open the front door, but he turned to Jose. "I'm going to get my brother off that porch and then I'm going to find those motherfuckers out there, whoever they are, and I'm going to kill them."

Jose started to say something, but he didn't. The look in Cole's eyes stopped him. He wasn't afraid of Cole, but he was wary of him. And there was a look in Cole's eyes like he'd never seen before.

"Wait, I'll help you," Jose said and he rushed back into the kitchen for another pair of dishwashing gloves.

Cole opened the front door, about to walk out onto the porch. But he froze, he stood very still as he stared at the front porch.

Jose rushed up behind Cole and saw what Cole was looking at. Jose just stared. "What the hell?" he whispered.

CHAPTER TWENTY-SIX

TREVOR'S HEAD AND the pieces of his body were gone. Cole stepped out onto the front porch, but only one step. He could hear Jose right behind him. "What the hell is this, Cole?"

Cole stared down at the floorboards of the porch. There were still puddles of blood all over the porch, some of the blood had turned a pinkish color as it mixed with the snow scattered across the floorboards. There were still splatters of blood on the front door and the front wall of the cabin where the pieces of Trevor's body had pelted the wood from whoever had thrown them.

But those pieces were gone now. The pieces *had* been here, Cole thought to himself. They hadn't been a figment of his imagination. Everyone else had seen them, too.

Jose rushed out through the doorway beside Cole. He took two more steps out onto the porch and looked around. "What the fuck?" he said. "What the fuck?!" he said a little louder. "How the hell …"

Cole looked around at the porch, then out at the snowy field and the trees in the distance. There was no one in the snowy field or the trees.

Jose looked around, his gun gripped in his hand that was sheathed in the rubber of dishwashing gloves. "Cole, somebody was out here just a few minutes ago picking up all of these pieces."

Cole didn't respond to Jose.

"How the hell didn't we hear them?"

Cole still didn't respond.

"How the fuck did they get up on this porch and take all of those … those pieces without us hearing them? Without us knowing."

Cole hurried over to the edge of the porch and looked over the railing. He stripped off the yellow dishwashing gloves and stuffed them into the pockets of his jacket. He dropped the box of garbage bags on the floorboards; it landed with a dull thud. He pulled his gun out of the waistband of his pants and studied the snow below the porch.

"Who the fuck *are* these people?" Cole heard Jose ask.

Cole walked along the edge of the porch, keeping close to the railing, his gun ready in his hand. He searched the snow with his eyes all the way around the porch. When he got to the other side, he looked back at Jose. "There aren't any tracks in the snow," he said.

"That can't be," Jose said in a low voice. "How the hell can they be doing this?"

Cole walked back to the porch steps that led down into the snow.

"Cole," Jose said. "What are you doing?"

Cole didn't answer.

"Hey, man. Why don't we just take the cases of money and walk out of here? We'll leave that girl and her kid here in the cabin, and we'll just walk on out of here. We don't have to hurt them; we'll tie them up and just leave them here."

"They'll die in there if we do that," Cole finally answered Jose as he stood at the edge of the steps.

"So," Jose spat out. "It's her friends out here doing this any-way. I'm sure they'll go inside the cabin and rescue her."

Cole descended the steps quickly down into the snow. He walked a few steps out into the snow which came up to mid-calf on him. He wore calf-high boots underneath his pants legs, but he could still feel the cold on his legs, creeping through the cloth, creeping into his flesh, into his bones. It was so cold out here that he could feel his lungs ache as he took breaths.

Jose followed Cole down into the snow. "Just the two of us," Jose said. "We don't even need Needles to leave with us. It's Needles' fault we're here in the first place."

Cole still didn't answer. He kept walking towards the corner of the cabin, away from the garage and Tom Gordon's ruined pickup truck parked in front of the garage doors which were still partway open. The garage made Cole think of the snowmobile he'd seen in there. It stayed in the back of his mind. He didn't want to tell Jose about it just yet.

You don't trust Jose enough to tell him about the snowmobile, Cole's mind whispered to him.

As if to prove Cole's point, Jose continued following Cole through the snow, trying to convince him to leave. "Come on, man. Just you and me. We could split the money fifty-fifty."

Cole stopped at the corner of the cabin and looked around at the fields of snow, at the line of trees that surrounded the fields. He didn't see any movement, he didn't hear anything. His eyes settled on the parting in the trees where the driveway began, the driveway that led back out to the county road.

God, it seemed like such a long time ago since they had come down that driveway in Stella's truck.

Cole took a step and then he took another step towards the driveway.

Frank's voice echoed in his mind. "He won't let you leave."

But Cole was going to walk to the driveway in the woods – at least that far. He had his gun ready. He was ready for these people to reveal themselves. He was ready to shoot them. He was ready to kill them. For Trevor.

Jose fell in beside Cole, matching Cole step for step through the snow as they trudged towards the driveway in the trees. Jose had given up trying to convince Cole to leave with him.

Maybe I should just leave by myself, Jose thought.

*

Inside the cabin, Stella and David sat on the couch. David was drawing again. Always drawing. She thought about the drawings she'd seen in his notebook. She had to talk to him about it, but she needed to wait for the right time. What he was drawing could be the answer to what was out there in the woods. But she didn't dare give herself too much hope.

She looked over at the recliner, at Needles. He had been hunched forward, his cross dangling down from his neck on the thin gold necklace as he stared down at the large Native American rug on the cabin floor. Something about the patterns and colors seemed to amaze Needles. He would spend hours staring at the patterns on the rug and rubbing the small cross on his necklace over and over again.

But now Needles looked at Stella and David.

And Stella realized that they were alone in the cabin with this lunatic. How long were Cole and Jose going to stay out there? She had seen that Trevor's body parts were gone, she had suspected that. And now Cole and Jose might be out there searching the woods for Trevor's killer.

They could be out there for a while, Stella thought. Maybe for hours.

Needles stood up quickly. He was a lanky man, but he was tall and all muscle, he had a wiry strength to him. But his eyes were the scariest part of him. They were lost, completely gone now. He had been going more and more crazy, and now he was all the way gone. Stella could see that; she had seen that same look in a man's eyes before – she'd seen it in New Mexico.

Needles smiled at them. "I believe you," he whispered to Stella. "They might not believe you," Needles gestured towards the front door, "but I know that there's something supernatural out there."

Stella didn't answer. She just watched Needles. She was ready to grab David and run from the couch to the front door if she needed to. The door was still ajar, letting the cold air into the cozy warmth of the cabin.

"It's okay, Stella," he said in a low voice, as a strange smile played at the corner of his lips. "I already know who's out there. It's the devil, isn't it? The old man in the bank told me."

Stella tensed and David stopped drawing as Needles took another step towards them with that insane smile still on his face.

Then Needles froze in mid-step when they heard the gunshots from outside.

*

Cole and Jose had only made it five more steps away from the cabin when the gunshots started. They ducked down, frozen for a moment as bullets whizzed past them and struck the logs of the cabin.

"Fuck!" Jose yelled.

They turned and ran as fast as they could through the snow as more shots were fired. Cole couldn't tell where the shots were coming from, somewhere from the woods, but he couldn't be sure exactly from where.

They made it to the steps of the porch and Cole turned and fired at the trees with his pistol, trying to provide some cover for them as they climbed the slippery steps up onto the porch that was still smeared with his brother's blood.

Needles was at the door as they made it up the steps. Needles fired his gun out at the woods, providing more cover.

"You see 'em?!" Jose shouted at Needles.

"No!" Needles yelled. He moved back into the cabin to allow Cole and Jose to duck inside as bullets pelted the thick logs of the cabin wall.

Cole closed the door and locked the locks, then he backed away from the door, his gun still in his hand. Jose hurried over to the window on the other side of the door that looked out onto the porch.

"You see anything?" Cole asked Jose.

Jose shook his head no. "Nothing."

"What kind of gun was it?" Needles asked, but they all were pretty sure they knew, it was a sound they'd heard plenty of times before. "I think it was a .45," Cole said, and then he uttered all of their thoughts. "It sounded like Frank's gun."

CHAPTER TWENTY-SEVEN

THREE O'CLOCK IN the morning. The half-full moon managed to shine some moonlight down onto the fields of snow and endless woods on the earth below, but clouds rolled through the night sky causing night shadows to glide across the trees, across the fields of snow, across the cabin.

Cole had downed at least ten cups of coffee. He'd made the coffee strong. He'd added a lot of sugar. He wanted to make sure that he was going to stay awake tonight.

Jose had opened the bottle of whiskey earlier in the night. He'd only sipped at it, catching a little bit of a buzz, not enough to make him drunk, but enough to give him some courage. And it was making him drowsy – Cole could see that. He could see that it was going to be up to him again to stay awake and on guard through the night.

David was the first one to fall asleep. He slept on top of his notebook, like his body was guarding it. Stella tried to pull it out from under his body, but every time she tried to move the notebook, David's eyes would pop open and he would stare at her with his large dark eyes.

"I'm just trying to make you more comfortable," she whispered to him.

But David held onto his notebook of drawings and slept on top of it.

Of course Stella could rip the notebook out of the little boy's hands if she wanted to, but she wasn't going to do that. She would talk to him about the things he'd drawn when it was the right time. In the meantime, her mind began to wander as she thought of different possibilities of what David's drawings could mean. Her archeologist's mind offered up different explanations, different scenarios, analyzing and studying.

Stella curled up next to David and eventually she closed her eyes and drifted off to sleep.

Needles fell asleep next, curled up in an uncomfortable position on the recliner that he sat in all the time. Cole told him earlier that he might wake him up in the morning to stand guard. But he wasn't sure if he was going to do that or not. He couldn't trust Needles anymore. And he wasn't sure if he could trust Jose either. He'd never been close to these guys; they were all criminals and their trust of each other only went so far. But Cole had trusted Trevor. And now the only person he really trusted was gone, the only one who would've had his back. His heart ached when he thought of Trevor. And a rage burned inside of him when he thought of Trevor's body (pieces) out there in the woods somewhere. His remains desecrated, scattered among the snow in the woods.

Cole made himself think of something else.

Jose sat next to Cole for a while at the dining room table, a small glass of whiskey in front of him. No drinking – that had always been one of Frank's rules when they were on a job together. After the job was done and they were about to go their separate ways, it was fine, but not while they were working. But Cole didn't say anything to Jose about it. They were way past working right now, and if a few sips of whiskey calmed Jose down, then Cole was thankful for that.

"What's our plan?" Jose asked in a low voice. The fire in him earlier was gone now. After they were shot at, Jose's idea of just walking out of here didn't seem so feasible.

"I don't know yet," Cole said and his thoughts turned once again to the snowmobile he'd seen tucked away under the blue tarp inside the free-standing garage. He could even feel the keys to the snowmobile in his pants pocket. There had to be some way he could get to it, see if it would start. There had to be some way to escape on it. But not right now. Not in the middle of the night.

"I'll tell you something," Jose said as he took another small sip of whiskey from his glass.

Cole didn't respond.

"If I see Frank again," Jose continued, "I'm going to get some answers out of him. I promise you that."

Cole didn't say anything.

Jose fell asleep a few hours later, stretching out on his blankets. He told Cole that he was just resting for a few minutes, but Cole heard him breathing heavily a few moments later, and then snoring lightly.

Cole sat at the dining room table and sipped his coffee. The only light on was over the stove, and the rest of the cabin was hidden in murky darkness. He glanced at the clock on the wall in the kitchen – three o'clock in the morning. He'd wait until dawn before he woke Jose up to take the next watch.

*

Needles woke up on the floor beside the recliner. It was late at night, he knew that, but he didn't know exactly what time it was. He sat up and suddenly he felt vulnerable on the floor. He didn't remember getting out of the chair and stretching out on the wood floor, but at some point in the night he must have.

Needles realized that something had woken him up, some kind of noise.

He looked back at the others. Everyone else was asleep. Even Cole and Jose were stretched out on their blankets on the floor, both of them breathing heavily. He was pretty sure that one of them was supposed to be standing guard through the night. But maybe they had given up on that, maybe they had realized what he had, that there was nothing they could do to fight back.

What kind of noise had it been that had woken him up? He tried to remember.

A thumping noise.

His eyes darted to the kitchen and Needles held his breath as he stared at the freezer against the far wall. The noise had come from the freezer, he was sure of it now. A thumping noise.

Thump.

The freezer lid popped up for a second, then it thumped back down, like someone inside was trying to push it open.

Like Tom Gordon was trying to get out.

Needles was frozen with fear. His throat had gone instantly dry, and all of his muscles seemed like they had turned to wet spaghetti. His lips trembled. He wanted to scream out to the others, he wanted to wake them up, but the only sound that would come out of his throat was a breathless wheeze.

It was silent in the cabin for a few moments and just when Needles began to think that maybe he'd been half asleep and still dreaming, the freezer lid flew open and smashed against the log wall of the cabin. The freezer was wide open.

Needles heard Tom Gordon before he actually saw him. He could hear the crackling sound of ice breaking, like the sound of ice cube trays being twisted to break the ice cubes free. Then Tom Gordon sat up in the freezer, he sat straight up like a vampire rising up out of his coffin.

Needles pushed himself back into the recliner, leaning against it, his hands clawing at the floor, searching his body and the floor for his gun. He tried to scream again, but only a whisper of sound would come out of his mouth. It was like being stuck in a nightmare where you tried to scream but no sound would come out, or you tried to run and the ax-wielding killer caught up anyway.

Tom Gordon turned his head to stare at Needles; the frozen flesh crackled with every move, his bluish skin sparkled with ice crystals. Even though Tom Gordon didn't have eyes anymore, he stared right at Needles like he could see him. And then Tom Gordon smiled.

Needles shook his head no. He tried to scream again, tried to plead with this thing that used to be the owner of this cabin. But he still couldn't utter a sound, and he still couldn't move. And he still couldn't find his gun.

Tom Gordon got out of the freezer faster than Needles would've expected. He crawled out, his bent limbs somehow cracking and straightening. It sounded like his bones were popping back into place.

Needles was finally able to move. He turned back to the others. One of them had to be awake by now, one of them had to have heard the freezer lid fly open and hit the wall, one of them had to have heard all of that crackling and popping of frozen flesh and bone.

Needles found his gun underneath the chair – he wasn't sure why it was under there, and he didn't have time to think about it right now. His fingers wrapped around the handle and he pulled it out and turned back to the kitchen, but he was suddenly face to face with Tom Gordon who was only inches away from him. Needles was sure that his heart was going to come to a stop, he was sure that his breath was going to dry up right in his lungs from fright. He stared at the bluish skin of Tom Gordon's face, the deep black holes where his eyes used to be. Tom Gordon's mouth opened, his mouth was a yawning black maw with jagged yellow teeth; his breath came out in a plume of frost as he whispered to Needles. "You know what to do. You know what needs to be done."

Needles snapped into action. He brought his gun up and fired. He squeezed the trigger over and over again, just shooting and shooting. He was on his feet without realizing it, holding his gun in both hands, trying to still his trembling arms as he squeezed off more rounds. He was screaming continuously without being aware of it.

The others woke up and jumped to their feet.

Cole was the first one at Needles' side, and Cole had his own gun in his hand, ready to shoot. "What is it?!" Cole yelled at Needles. "What's going on?!"

Needles pulled the trigger again and again, but the gun only clicked. He was out of ammo.

Cole aimed his gun into the kitchen where Needles had been shooting; he stared into the kitchen which was lit up somewhat by the light over the stove. There were bullet holes in the logs of the far wall, and two bullets in the freezer. But Cole didn't see anyone in the kitchen; he didn't see what Needles had been shooting at. "What was it?" he asked Needles.

"It was the guy from the freezer," Needles finally whispered in a trembling voice.

"Tom Gordon?"

"Yeah," Needles answered. "He got out of the freezer."

CHAPTER TWENTY-EIGHT

"NEEDLES," COLE SAID in a gentle voice. "Put your gun down."

Needles kept his gun aimed at the kitchen even though there were no more bullets in the clip. His arms trembled as he aimed his gun at the freezer. "I saw him, Cole. I saw him get out of that freezer."

"Needles, lower your gun. Let me take it. We don't want any accidents."

Needles did not lower his gun.

Stella and David sat up on the couch. Jose stood on his bedroll, his gun down at his side; his eyes were puffy, and he swayed just a bit from the buzz of the whiskey a few hours earlier, and from exhaustion. He looked into the kitchen; he looked at the bullet holes on the wall and at the two bullet holes in the freezer, which was now leaking water from underneath it. Jose looked back at Cole and Needles.

"Needles," Cole said again, his voice lower and firmer. "Lower your weapon."

Needles finally lowered his gun, but it was more out of sheer exhaustion than from Cole's orders. He looked at Cole with red-rimmed eyes. Tears slipped out of the corners of his eyes. "You don't believe me, do you?"

"I didn't say that, Needles. Let me see your gun. We don't want another accident. Remember the old man in the bank?"

Needles nodded as he let out a shuddering breath. He handed his gun to Cole.

Cole took the gun and shoved it into the waistband of his pants. He felt a little relieved now that Needles didn't have a weapon. He planned on getting all of the extra clips Needles had for the gun, but not right now.

Needles looked back at the kitchen and wiped at the snot and tears on his face. "Go look, Cole," he said as he stared at the freezer. "Go look and see if that guy's still in there."

"It was just a nightmare," Cole said in a soothing voice. "We're all scared and tired. Stressed out. You just had a – "

"No, Cole!" Needles screamed at him and he looked at him with wide frightened eyes. "It wasn't a fucking nightmare. I know what I saw. It was that guy, Tom Gordon; he sat up in the freezer. I saw him get out and walk towards me."

"Maybe you were still half asleep," Cole offered, trying to keep his cool. "Maybe your eyes were open, but you were still dreaming. That happens. Especially when people are very tired and stressed out."

Needles shook his head no. "I know what I saw."

Cole looked at Jose and gestured for Jose to check out the freezer.

As Jose went to the kitchen, Cole looked at Stella and David. "You two see anything?"

They both shook their heads no.

"Nothing to say?" Cole asked Stella.

Stella shook her head no.

Jose stood in front of the freezer, his gun still in his hand. He opened the freezer lid and looked down inside.

"Is he still in there?" Needles asked Jose, on the verge of tears again, panic in his voice.

Jose looked back at Cole. "Cole, come over here."

"Is he in there?!" Needles screamed.

"Yes, damn it!" Jose yelled at Needles, but he looked at Cole. "Cole?"

Cole hurried across the wood floor to the kitchen. He still had his gun in his hand, and he could feel the heat from Needles' pistol shoved down in the waistband of his pants. He stood beside Jose and looked down at Tom Gordon's body. He was still in the freezer, but his body looked different. It looked like he was in a different position, and some of the ice that had covered his body before looked cracked now.

Cole and Jose looked at each other, but they didn't say anything out loud and Cole was thankful for that, he didn't want to hear Needles ranting and raving again. Something seemed strange about this, but Cole was a rational man who didn't believe in the supernatural. His mind was already coming up with possibilities. Maybe they had forgotten exactly what position Tom Gordon had been in when they saw him the first time. Maybe the bullets from Needles' gun had shattered the ice all over Tom Gordon's body. It had to be something like that, Cole thought, something rational.

Jose shut the lid. They glanced at each other but didn't say anything. Cole noticed a gash in the log wall behind the freezer; it looked like it was from the freezer lid being slammed into the wall. But it could've been there before and they just noticed it now.

Cole looked down at the kitchen floor and noticed ice chips and crystals all over the floor, but the water leaking from the freezer was reaching out for the ice chips and melting them. Cole looked away.

Needles was having a waking nightmare, Cole thought. That's all. He woke up from a nightmare and panicked, and then he started shooting. Cole had taken Needles' gun, and that was the right thing to do for now.

Cole turned back to the others. "Tom Gordon's still in the freezer. Needles just had a nightmare."

"It wasn't a fucking nightmare," Needles mumbled to himself as he crawled back into the safety of his recliner.

Cole glanced at the clock on the kitchen wall. It was almost sunup.

*

As the sun climbed the morning sky, nearing the tops of the trees and shedding its light across the blankets of snow on the ground, Cole sat at the dining room table. He'd made more coffee. He made it even stronger. He added even more sugar.

The others had stayed awake for a little bit, but then one by one they had fallen back asleep.

Except Stella.

She walked into the kitchen and poured herself a cup of coffee. She sat down in a chair diagonally from Cole, her back to the others who slept in the living room.

Cole glanced at her, but he didn't feel like questioning her. She wasn't going to answer him anyway and he was tired of it. He was tired of all of this. His nerves were fried and he was just tired.

"I'm sorry," Stella whispered to Cole.

He turned and looked at her.

"About Trevor. I didn't know he was your brother at first. I should've seen the resemblance. I'm sorry about what happened to him."

Cole nodded. She seemed sincere, but he couldn't be sure with her anymore.

"I don't know what's out there," she told him. "I swear to you, that's the truth."

Cole just stared at her.

"What did you see in that freezer?" she asked in a low voice, almost a whisper. She turned and looked into the living room at the others for just a moment, and then she looked at Cole again.

"Tom Gordon's in that freezer," Cole told her. "That's where he's been the whole time. Needles had a nightmare and freaked out."

Stella stared at Cole for a long moment and then she just nodded.

"Why won't you tell me everything that happened down at that dig site in New Mexico?"

Stella thought it over for a moment. "I want to trust you. But I don't know if I can."

Cole just stared at Stella for a long moment. There was nothing he could do or say to make her trust him now. She had been right earlier when she asked how he could ask for her help after carjacking her and David and pointing a weapon at their faces.

"Frank will be back," Stella whispered, catching Cole off guard a little. He stared at her.

"He's going to ask for something else," Stella continued, "and you have to give him what he asks for, no matter what it is, or someone else will be taken."

A sudden anger flared up inside of Cole. "And you're just telling me this now? Why didn't you tell us this before, when Frank asked for the money? If we would've known to put the money out there, then maybe Trevor would still be alive."

"You wouldn't have believed me if I would've told you before, and you know it," Stella answered Cole through clenched teeth. Her eyes burned into Cole's eyes.

Cole sighed, whether he wanted to admit it to her or not, he knew she was right.

"He still wants the money?" Cole asked Stella in a whisper.

"He doesn't want the money. It doesn't have anything to do with the money. It never did. He wants things and you have to give them to him no matter what they are."

Cole stared at Stella. "What is he going to ask for next?"

Stella stared back, but she didn't answer.

"You know, don't you?" Cole whispered. "You know what he's going to ask for next."

Stella jumped as someone touched the back of her neck. She whirled around in her chair and she was face to face with David.

She hadn't even heard him walk up behind her from the living room.

And Cole hadn't seen David walk up behind Stella.

David stared at Stella and Cole. "He's outside again. He's calling you."

CHAPTER TWENTY-NINE

COLE WOKE JOSE and Needles up. Jose jumped to his feet and claimed he'd only been asleep for a few minutes. Cole didn't want to argue with him.

"What time is it?" Jose asked as he struggled to come fully awake.

"About ten o'clock," Cole answered as he slipped on his leather gloves.

Cole put his coat on and zipped it up. He checked his gun.

Needles jumped up from his recliner. "I'm not going out there again," he said. He looked at Cole. "I want my gun back."

"Not right now, Needles," Cole said and looked at Stella. "Get your coat on, I want you out there with us this time."

Stella stared at Cole. "I'll get David's coat."

"Leave him inside this time. Needles will keep an eye on him."

"I'd rather not let David out of my sight," Stella said.

Cole didn't say anything – he wasn't giving her a suggestion.

"I'll watch him," Needles said and then he glanced at the front door. He seemed to be trying to be helpful, but Stella could see something else in Needles' eyes, something buried deep inside there, something sinister.

Jose's words from last night echoed through Cole's mind – "If I see Frank again, I'm going to get some answers out of him. I promise you that." Cole didn't want David outside if Jose started shooting at Frank and Frank or whoever else was out there in the woods decided to shoot back. But he didn't want to go into a long explanation about it with Stella.

Stella got her coat on and she walked over to David who sat rigidly on the couch, his spiral notebook on his lap. She crouched down in front of him and smoothed his long hair back. She looked into his dark eyes. She could see the fear in those eyes. "You sit right here," she whispered to David. "Don't come outside no matter what you hear. Okay?"

David just nodded.

"We'll only be out there for a few minutes."

Again David nodded. Stella hugged him, and then she stood up and looked at Needles. She didn't have a good feeling about leaving David in here with him, but she could be back inside in a few seconds if she needed to. At least Needles didn't have his gun with him anymore.

Cole, Jose, and Stella gathered at the front door, bracing themselves for a moment before Cole unlocked and opened the door. Cole and Jose checked their guns again, making sure they had full clips and making sure a bullet was chambered and ready. Cole had reloaded Needles' gun and he had it stuck into the back of the waistband of his pants. He had Trevor's gun in his coat pocket.

Cole glanced at Stella. She had been about to tell him a few minutes ago what Frank was going to ask for – but now he was going to find out for himself.

Cole unlocked the door. He opened the door. He stepped out onto the front porch. Jose and Stella followed him, and the three of them stood close to each other on the porch. Stella closed the door, but she left it open just a crack. She didn't want to shut the door all the way, and she wanted to be close to the door.

The three of them stared out at Frank who stood in the same spot in the snow as before. He looked the same, same blue flannel shirt, same pants, same unanimated face, his head cocked to the side at an odd angle. He looked like a puppet waiting for his strings to be pulled.

Frank came alive, and that creepy smile was on his face in an instant. "Hi, everyone!" he shouted and gave them a mechanical-like wave of his hand.

"What did you do with Trevor?" Cole shouted.

Frank's smile drooped and his face dropped in an exaggerated frown. "Oh, that was unfortunate," he told them.

"What did you do with his body?!" Cole yelled.

"You have to give him what he wants!" Frank said with the frown still on his face. "You have to give him exactly what he wants or bad things will happen."

"We're not doing anything anymore until you tell me what you did with Trevor!"

Frank stood motionless in the snow, his head cocked to the side, almost like he was listening to something no one else could hear. "You really want to see Trevor again?" Frank asked.

"Yes, right now! Where is he?!"

But Frank didn't answer.

"Who is doing this? Why doesn't this person come out and show himself?!" Cole yelled; he could feel the rage building up inside of him again, he felt like he was going to snap at any second. "I want to see him!!"

"You wouldn't understand," Frank said. "It has to be this way."

"I want to speak to this person directly!" Cole said.

"You are," Frank answered. "Through me."

Cole could tell that Jose was getting antsy beside him, fidgeting, ready to go for his gun. "This is bullshit," Jose whispered. "Let's just rush him. Make him talk."

"What do you want?!" Cole yelled out to Frank

Frank stood motionless in the snow, impervious to the freezing weather even though he only wore pants and a flannel shirt.

"He wants two human eyeballs on the front porch by sundown," Frank told them.

*

Inside the cabin, Needles sat at the edge of his recliner, his elbows on his knees like he was ready to pop up onto his feet at any second. He was on edge, like he needed to get up and move, like he had something important he needed to do very soon.

And he *did* have something important to do.

What he'd seen last night had been no nightmare – it had been real. And he'd been given instructions. He knew what he needed to do. Maybe if he did what the devil told him to do, then the devil would let him go.

David sat on the couch, his notebook beside him. He wasn't drawing right now; he was watching every move that Needles made.

Needles glanced at the front door. He could see that it was still slightly ajar. He thought about getting up and closing the door, and then locking it. He could lock them outside with the devil that they didn't believe in.

Needles jumped to his feet. He only had a short time to accomplish his task, and he couldn't waste time running for the door, it might spook the kid and he would run for the door or run to the back or scream. Instead of walking to the door, Needles walked into the kitchen. He glanced at the freezer for a second. He could imagine Tom Gordon's body thawing inside the leaking freezer.

A thought occurred to Needles: maybe Tom Gordon *wasn't* a demon, maybe he had been sent by God to give Needles a message. Maybe Needles was the only one who could see, maybe Needles was the only one who could carry out God's plan. God had given Needles a warning through the old man in the bank, and Needles hadn't meant to shoot the old man; he was truly sorry about that, he didn't even remember pulling the trigger.

But now maybe Needles was getting a second chance. God

was giving him a second chance to carry out this mission. Maybe the demon wasn't out there; maybe the demon has been inside with them all along – the demon was David. And Tom Gordon had been sent to tell Needles what to do, to kill this demon.

Needles rubbed the gold crucifix that hung around his neck. He opened the kitchen drawer and rummaged around until he found the biggest kitchen knife he could find.

Needles turned and walked into the living room. He watched David who stared at him. David saw the knife in his hand, Needles was sure of that, but David didn't try to run for the front door, or even try to scream. That had to mean David was a demon, and that was proof enough for Needles.

Thank you, God, Needles whispered in his mind. Thank you for giving me this chance to carry out your wishes.

So crafty the devil was, Needles thought, hiding inside such an innocent-looking child. Nobody would ever suspect what this child really was. But Needles could tell, Needles could see. Oh yes, he could see right through David.

Needles walked towards the couch, the knife in his hand; he didn't even bother to try and hide it now. The light from the windows winked off the long blade of the knife. David just watched him with his large dark eyes. David knew what was coming, Needles was certain. And David knew that he couldn't win. Evil couldn't fight goodness – it was no match for it.

When Needles stepped onto the area rug, the Native American rug with its colorful patterns, David suddenly got to his feet; he glanced at the front door, but he didn't run for it, he just looked back at Needles like he was frozen with fright.

Needles smiled at David. "You know what I have to do, don't you?"

CHAPTER THIRTY

"EYEBALLS?!" JOSE YELLED out in disgust at Frank. Jose stood on the front porch, his hand itching to draw his gun and run out into the snow and charge Frank. But for a few seconds he was too shocked to move, he could only stare at Frank. "Eyeballs?" he spat out again. "What the fuck?"

"You have to give him what he wants," Frank said, and that plastic smile was back on his face.

Jose jumped off the porch and down into the snow; Cole didn't even have a chance to stop him. Jose ran through the snow right at Frank as he howled a scream of fury.

Cole raised his gun, aiming it at Frank, ready to cover Jose.

But there were no shots fired at them from the trees.

And Frank wasn't turning to run. He wasn't pulling out his pistol. He wasn't doing anything except waiting patiently and motionless as Jose ran right at him.

Jose reached Frank, his gun aimed right at Frank's head. If anyone was going to start firing at him from the woods, Jose thought, then he was going to make damn sure that he blew Frank's head off first. Frank watched Jose with no expression in his eyes, that plastic smile on his face. Jose wanted to smash his face in with the butt of his gun; he wanted to wipe that stupid smile away.

Jose stood in front of Frank, his gun aimed at his face, at that stupid grin. "You're coming back inside, motherfucker," Jose growled, and he moved around to the back of Frank to march him to the cabin. "You're going to give us some fucking answers. You're going to …"

Jose's words died in his throat when he got around to the back of Frank. There was nothing there – no back to Frank at all. It looked like Frank's back had been sliced off and his torso had been scooped out – muscles, bones, organs, blood, all of it gone. He was completely hollow inside. Even part of the back of Frank's head was gone and the inside of his head was hollow. There were only the glistening red walls of flesh inside of his hollowed-out body.

Jose couldn't understand what he was seeing. Frank couldn't be alive. No one could be alive like this.

Cole stood at the edge of the porch, his gun still aimed at Frank. He was ready for the barrage of gunfire to begin from the woods, but nothing happened, nobody was shooting. There was no wall of snow, no sudden blizzard, nothing.

But something was wrong with Jose. He had gotten behind Frank to march him back to the cabin, but then he stopped cold, staring at the back of Frank in horror. At what? What had he seen?

Cole heard a sharp inhale from Stella. He managed a quick glance at her, and he saw her body stiffen, her eyes on Frank. Did she know what had stopped Jose? Did she know what Jose was seeing?

"Jose!" Cole shouted, trying to break his paralysis.

But Jose wasn't listening, he wasn't moving, he wasn't answering. He only stared at the back of Frank.

Cole was about to jump down into the snow, but then Jose stumbled back around to the front of Frank, staring at him.

Jose moved back around to face Frank. His gun hand had dropped down to his side, and his body had weakened so much that he barely held onto his gun. He stared at Frank's face.

Frank was still smiling. He spoke, and when he spoke Jose could now see the barest traces of light coming through his mouth from his hollowed-out head. "Go," Frank whispered to Jose. "Go back and tell the others what you've seen. Tell them that they have to give him what he wants. There is no other way."

Jose took a step back, then another. Then another. He backed up through the snow, away from Frank, but he didn't take his eyes off of Frank.

Frank just stood there in the snow, still smiling, his head still cocked to the side.

After five backwards steps through the deep snow, Jose turned and ran for the cabin. He'd never been this frightened in his life. He never knew anyone could experience terror like this. He ran in a blind panic. He ran towards the only safety left that he knew of right now – the cabin. But even in his white-hot panic, he knew that the cabin wasn't safe anymore. Nowhere was safe anymore.

Jose stumbled up the porch steps, gibbering, not even sure what he was saying, not sure what he was thinking, everything was just a blur of white panic. It was like his brain had seen something so horrible and unimaginable that it was beginning to shut down.

Cole helped Jose up the steps. Jose's gun slipped from his fingers and clunked down onto the floorboards of the porch. Cole picked up the gun while still holding on to Jose.

"What's wrong, Jose?" Cole asked. He could hear the panic in his own voice. "What did you see?"

"He … he … he's not …" Jose stammered. He couldn't get the words out. "Insides …" he whispered.

Just then they heard a scream from inside the cabin – David's scream.

"David!" Stella yelled and she bolted for the front door.

CHAPTER THIRTY-ONE

S TELLA RUSHED INSIDE to see Needles chasing David with a gigantic kitchen knife. Needles sliced the knife down through the air, stabbing at David. But David managed to duck out of the way of the deadly swing just in time.

Stella didn't even think about it, she rushed right at Needles and slammed into him.

Needles was thrown off balance from both surprise and because Stella had hit him that hard.

"NOOO!!!" Stella screamed as she tackled Needles and drove him back into his recliner. They both fell over the recliner and Stella heard the satisfactory sound of the knife clattering to the floor.

Cole was inside the cabin right after Stella. He saw Needles try to stab David with the knife, but Stella had reacted a split second before Cole had, and he watched her tackle Needles over the recliner. Both of them fell to a heap on the floor on the other side of the recliner and Cole was sure at least one of them had fallen on the knife, but then he heard it drop on the floor

Jose stumbled inside the cabin and shut the door. He fumbled with the lock with his shaking hands. He knew the locks wouldn't hold back whatever was out there, but he locked the door anyway. He stumbled over to the dining room table, oblivious to the fight in the living room between Stella and Needles. Jose plopped down in one of the dining room chairs as his mind replayed what he'd seen out there in the snow – Frank's hollowed-out body.

On the floor beside the recliner, Needles kicked Stella off of him. He had been surprised by her strength, caught off guard for a moment, but Needles was stronger than she was and his kick sent her through the air where she landed on the Native American rug in the center of the room. Needles rolled over in a quick movement and grabbed the dropped knife from the floor.

As Stella struggled back to her feet, Cole shot across her vision like a blur of movement. She watched Cole punch Needles in the jaw as he tried to stand up. In less than two seconds Cole hit Needles again and again in the face until he dropped the knife.

Cole tackled Needles, who was already woozy from the punches to his face, and then he drove him into the wall. They both slid down the wall to the floor as pictures crashed from the wall to the floor all around them. Needles fell over onto his stomach, and before Needles had a chance to turn over, Cole crawled on top of his back like an MMA fighter; he held him face-down as he wrenched one of Needles' arms behind his back and held it there. Needles wailed out in pain.

"Get me something to tie his hands with!" Cole yelled at Jose.

But Jose wasn't listening. He stared down at the table, his mind tuning out everything around him. He kept seeing Frank's body in his mind's eye, his hollow body, the red and glistening walls of flesh inside of his torso and head.

Stella jumped up from the floor. Her stomach hurt from where Needles had kicked her, but she could tell there was no serious damage. She ran to the kitchen counter and grabbed the balled-up telephone cord Cole had tossed there what seemed like so long ago. She grabbed it and ran back to Cole.

"Tie it around his wrist!" Cole screamed at Stella.

Needles tried to fight back, but he couldn't buck Cole off of his back. Cole had a handful of Needles' hair in his other hand and he slammed Needles' face down onto the wood floor, nearly knocking him out, definitely dazing him for a moment.

Stella tied the cord tightly around Needles' wrist, a double knot.

"Hold the cord," Cole told her as he grabbed Needles' other arm. Needles tried to struggle, but he was too dazed and Cole was too strong. Cole brought Needles' wrists together and he didn't even have to tell Stella what to do – she wrapped the cord around both wrists several times and tied it tight.

Cole tested the bonds and after he was satisfied that they were tight, he sat back on his butt on the floor as Needles writhed beside him and worked his way up into a sitting position, his back and bound hands against the wall. There were tears in Needles' eyes and blood trickled from his nose down into his mouth. "You don't understand," he told Cole. "I had to do it. I had to."

"Shut up," Cole said as he exhaled a long breath.

"David," Stella whispered. She ran over to the couch but David wasn't there. "David!" she called out. She went to the end of the couch and found David crouched down beside the end of it, hiding from Needles. He looked up at her with his dark eyes full of fear.

She dropped down to her knees and reached out for him. "It's okay," she told him. "He's tied up now. He won't get you."

David jumped into her arms and hugged her.

Stella cried as David held onto her. "I'm sorry," she said. "I'm sorry I left you in here with him. I should've known."

David pulled away from Stella and he nodded at her. "It's okay," he told her in his soft voice. He smiled. "I'm okay now."

Stella let out a laugh even though she was still crying a little bit. She wiped away at her tears. She looked him over quickly even though he told her he was okay; she didn't see any wounds of any kind on him. "You're not hurt anywhere, are you?"

"No. I'm okay."

Stella exhaled a deep breath. "Thank God."

Cole watched Stella and David for a moment, and then he

looked at Needles who was still sitting against the wall. Needles looked at Cole with his tear-streaked face. "You don't understand what's going on here, Cole. That kid's a demon. He's doing all of this on his own. He's not a child, he's a monster."

"Shut up, Needles."

"He's the devil. He's the one you should be afraid of, not me."

"I swear to God, Needles, if you don't shut the fuck up ..." Cole let his words trail off.

Needles became very quiet and suddenly calm. A strange smile appeared on his face. "You'll see," he whispered to Cole. "You'll see soon enough."

Cole walked away from Needles – he had to get away from him or he was afraid he was going to hit him again. Besides, Cole had another concern at this moment – Jose.

He walked over to Jose and stared at him.

Jose sat in the dining room table chair, his body slouched, his eyes distant, his head hung down.

"Jose," Cole said in a soft voice. He pulled out a chair and moved it over so that he sat down right in front of Jose.

Jose didn't respond.

"Jose!" Cole said a little louder.

Jose looked at Cole. "We have to give him what he wants," Jose said in an emotionless voice. "We have to give him anything he asks for."

"What's wrong, Jose?" Cole asked. "What did you see out there?"

"Frank's not real," Jose said, and then he thought for a moment. "He's not alive. He can't be."

"What do you mean?"

"There's nothing inside of Frank anymore."

"Nothing inside?"

"He's been hollowed out," Jose said quickly. "He's like some ... some kind of puppet. His back has been torn off and something scooped out all of his insides. Everything's gone. There's nothing in there."

"Then how – "

"I don't know!" Jose snapped. He shook his head. "I don't know," he repeated in a softer voice. "He's just a puppet for whatever's out there."

Cole glanced at Stella; she had taken David to the couch and sat him down. David grabbed his notebook and pen right away, and he held them protectively on his lap. They both looked back at Cole and Jose.

Jose startled Cole by grabbing his arm hard, Jose's fingers dug into Cole's flesh. But Cole didn't pull away; he stared into Jose's unblinking eyes of terror. "We have to give him the eyeballs. We have to give them to him."

CHAPTER THIRTY-TWO

"IT CAN DO anything it wants to," Jose continued as he stared into Cole's eyes.

"No it can't," Cole answered him, "or we'd all be dead already. If this thing can come in here anytime it wants to and take all of us, then why hasn't this ... this thing done that yet?"

Jose startled Cole by jumping to his feet. He paced around for a few seconds, like he wasn't sure where he was going to go or what he was going to do, he was like a caged animal that knew it couldn't escape but couldn't help running around the cage and searching for a way out. Jose dashed to the kitchen and grabbed the bottle of whiskey off the counter. He spun the lid off and drank down a few long swallows of the bourbon, something to numb him from the horrors that waited outside for them.

Cole watched Jose for a few seconds, but he knew he wasn't going to be able to get through to Jose right now – he was too frightened by whatever he'd seen out there, by Frank's hollowed-out body? Cole couldn't believe that, he couldn't wrap his mind around that. It had to be a mistake; Jose had to have misunderstood what he'd seen out there. There was no way that could be possible. This couldn't be happening. This couldn't be real.

Cole looked over at Stella, and then he walked towards her. "Why eyeballs?" he asked her. "If all this ... thing that's supposed to be out there wants is eyeballs, then why doesn't it take Frank's eyeballs?" Cole hesitated for a second before finishing the rest of his sentence, like it was painful to get the words out. "Or Trevor's."

Stella stared at him with unwavering eyes. "Because it wants us to do it."

"Why? Why would someone want us to do this?"

Stella didn't answer, and Cole could see that she wasn't going to answer. She was guarding some of the information, Cole could see that now. And in a way, he couldn't blame her. But he didn't think she was hiding things because she was a part of what was going on out there, more like she knew who was out there and she was strategizing to save David and herself.

Cole sighed. Eyeballs. They couldn't just take someone's eyeballs, could they? And whose eyeballs? Cole wasn't going to volunteer. Neither was Jose. Cole would not allow them to take Stella or David's eyes. That only left one possibility.

Cole glanced at Needles.

For a moment he thought about Tom Gordon in the freezer – they could take his eyeballs. But his eyes were already gone. Like this thing was one step ahead of them, like it had taken Tom Gordon's eyeballs so they couldn't use them now.

They all heard a sound on the front porch.

All of them stared at the front door.

Outside, on the front porch, there were heavy footsteps walking across the wooden porch to the front door.

The footsteps stopped.

Three loud knocks on the front door.

Cole glanced at Stella. "Who is it?" he whispered.

Stella shook her head no, indicating that she didn't know who it was.

"Frank?" Cole whispered.

This time Stella shook her head no – her eyes said that it wasn't Frank.

Jose set the bottle of whiskey down on the edge of the counter; he almost let it tip over and fall to the floor, but he slid it back slowly from the edge so it wouldn't fall, he did all of this without looking at the bottle, still staring at the front door the whole time.

Jose didn't go for his gun. He didn't move towards the door either. He was frozen with fear; he just stared at the front door with wide eyes.

Needles squirmed against the wall, trying to squirm his way closer to the recliner, he was almost behind the recliner now, trying to hide behind it, but he still peeked at the door from behind the piece of furniture. He was whimpering.

Three more knocks at the door. The door seemed to shake in its frame from the knocks.

"You have to untie me, Cole," Needles hissed. "You can't leave me like this."

Cole ignored Needles; he took a step towards the door and pulled his gun out from the waistband of his pants.

"Cole, please ..." Needles begged, beginning to cry.

The door handle rattled like whoever was on the other side was trying to turn the locked handle, trying to get in.

Cole took another step towards the door, his gun ready. He was close to the door now, about to reach out and open the door. The jiggling of the door handle stopped – only silence from the other side of the door for a moment.

"Cole, wait," Jose said with a tremor running through his voice. Jose still hadn't moved from his spot by the kitchen counter.

Then Cole heard the person speak from behind the door. "Cole," the person said. The voice was deep and guttural, yet Cole still recognized the voice, it was the voice of his little brother – Trevor's voice.

Trevor was out there. But that couldn't be. Trevor was dead, he'd seen it, he'd seen the pieces of his body, his decapitated head sitting in the middle of the porch like a trophy.

"Help me, Cole," Trevor whispered from the other side of the door.

Maybe he hadn't really seen the pieces of Trevor's body, his mind whispered. Maybe it hadn't been real. Maybe all of this is some kind of nightmare that he can't wake up from.

Cole rushed to the door and unlocked the deadbolt and then he unlocked the door handle. He grabbed the door handle which wasn't rattling anymore, like the person (Trevor) on the other side, was waiting for him to open it, waiting for Cole to invite him in.

"Cole ..." Stella whispered.

But Cole didn't hear her.

Cole opened the door and screamed without realizing it when he saw what stood on the front porch.

CHAPTER THIRTY-THREE

TREVOR STOOD ON the front porch; the pieces of his body had been put back together, the pieces stacked back up into what resembled a human body again, but the pieces were not fitting back together too well, the pieces didn't quite line up with each other anymore. In the deep lines where the pieces met each other, tatters of bloody clothing hung in ragged strips.

Trevor's head sat on his neck at a strange, cocked angle, a little like Frank's head. His face was slack, his eyes glassy, his skin pale. His yawning mouth moved, and his muscles creaked as he tried to work his mouth closed and then open again, trying to speak, trying to utter out words through vocal chords that must have been severed.

"Give him what he wants, Cole," the monstrosity that used to be Cole's brother grunted out.

Cole had screamed when he'd first seen this thing that used to be his brother. But now he stood only a few feet away from this impossibility and he couldn't move for a moment, frozen with fear, with awe, with confusion. His mind reeled and everything faded away around him for a moment. He had been aware for a few seconds that Needles was screaming from behind him somewhere. And Jose was shouting something at him, maybe to shut the door or shoot, Cole wasn't sure what he said because everything was fading away into darkness all around him.

And the darkness was closing in – he could feel his mind slowing, his chest heaving, his muscles weakening.

He was very close to passing out.

Trevor took a step forward and the pieces of his legs that had been stuck back together shifted and moved, and there was not only the creaking sound of stiff muscles trying to work together, but the wet pulpy sound of meat squishing against meat.

This isn't possible, Cole's mind whispered. There's no way this thing should be able to move.

Trevor's mouth hung open impossibly wide like the jaw had been dislocated and then shoved back into his face, and now it was off-center. His mouth opened and then snapped shut again and then opened once more, like he was trying to say something else. "Cole ..."

Cole couldn't listen to anything else this thing had to say.

This wasn't his brother anymore.

This wasn't Trevor.

This thing that used to be his brother stumbled forward and reached for Cole.

Cole aimed his gun at the monstrosity and he pulled the trigger over and over again; five shots into the head and torso of this thing. The bullets knocked the reanimated thing back a few steps and tore large chunks out of what used to be Trevor.

Cole screamed again as he kicked the door shut and lunged for the door; he locked the door handle with trembling fingers, and then the deadbolt. He backed away from the door, staring at it.

Needles was still screaming. "It can get inside! It can get inside anytime it wants to! It can do anything it wants to us!"

Cole turned and stared at Needles with dead eyes – eyes that had seen too much horror and now those eyes were dead calm. "Shut up," he told Needles in a soft voice.

Needles snapped his mouth shut as he stared at Cole from the side of the recliner where he cowered.

Jose still stood right next to the counter, he hadn't moved an inch the whole time. He watched Cole. "That wasn't Trevor anymore, Cole."

Cole walked towards Jose with slow, deliberate steps.

"You know that, right, Cole? That wasn't Trevor anymore, just like that's not Frank anymore out there."

Cole walked right up to Jose, his gun still gripped in his right hand.

"Cole, put the gun away," Jose said in a low voice. He reached behind him and grabbed the bottle of whiskey from off the counter. He handed the bottle to Cole with a trembling hand. "Here, take a sip, man."

Cole stood very still for a second, his eyes still dead, his breathing still shallow, his face slack with shock. Then he shoved his gun down into his waistband and took the bottle of whiskey from Jose. He took two long swallows of the fiery liquid.

Jose glanced at the clock on the kitchen wall, and then he looked back at Cole who still gripped the whiskey bottle by the neck. "It's getting late. Maybe only a few hours before sundown."

Cole just nodded – Jose didn't need to explain what he meant. They only had a short amount of time to decide what they were going to do. He glanced over at Stella and David who sat on the couch, both sitting up ramrod straight, like they might bolt any second. But where would they go? Where *could* they go?

Stella stared at Cole, and she slowly nodded her head. "It will keep coming back," she said in a low voice.

Cole took one more swig of the whiskey, and then screwed the lid back on. He handed the bottle back to Jose as he stared at Stella. "I want you and David to go into Tom Gordon's bedroom. I don't want David out here when we do this."

Needles pushed himself away from the recliner, his eyes were bugging out. He shook his head no, his arms struggling behind his back, trying to wriggle out of his bonds, but they were tied too tightly.

"No, Cole, please."

Cole ignored Needles. He'd made his decision. It had to be Needles. He'd killed the old man at the bank which was the reason they were here. And he'd tried to kill David. If they had to take someone's eyeballs, then it had to be Needles.

Needles kicked his legs wildly on the floor, beginning to cry and scream. "Please, Cole. We don't have to do this! We can think of something else!"

Cole didn't look at Needles. He looked at Stella and David and nodded at them, gesturing at them to go to the bedroom.

Stella stood up and took David's hand. David had the notebook tucked under his arm. They walked across the living room and gave Needles a wide berth. Stella glanced at Needles who had thrashed his way away from the recliner and more towards the middle of the living room, onto the Native American rug that he stared at for such long periods of time. His face was wet with tears, his skin red from the exertion of thrashing, his eyes wild with fear as he looked around at the cabin like this would be the last thing in the world that he'd ever see.

Stella and David walked to the bedroom. They would be alone in the bedroom and this was going to be her chance to talk to David about what she'd seen in his notebook.

CHAPTER THIRTY-FOUR

COLE CHECKED THE windows of Tom Gordon's bedroom as Stella and David made themselves comfortable on the lumpy, unmade bed. The windows were still locked and Cole didn't see anything moving out there in the snow. But he wanted to check. He didn't like the idea of leaving Stella and David by themselves in the bedroom, but he didn't want David in the living room watching him and Jose take out Needles' eyeballs.

And Cole had a feeling that nothing was going to happen to any of them as long as they were following the instructions, as long as they were giving it what it wanted.

Cole couldn't dwell on the idea of what was out there making them do this for too long or that darkness would begin to creep in from all around him, that darkness that invited him to just close his eyes and float away from all of this.

"We'll be okay," Stella said as she stared at Cole. "It won't come for us right now," she told him, confirming what he had just been thinking.

"I don't know how long this will take," he told her. "We have to find some rope or tape and get him ... get him ready."

"As long as it's done by sundown," Stella reminded him.

Cole nodded as a wave of nausea wormed its way through his guts. He could feel bile at the back of his throat. This couldn't be happening, he thought. But it *was* happening and they needed to hurry.

He left the room in a hurry. He closed the door and Stella could hear him stomping down the hall.

Stella turned to David who watched the door for a moment, clutching his spiral notebook which had become a little tattered at the edges now from him sleeping with it and protecting it the whole time.

But Stella had seen what he'd been drawing, and she needed to confront him about it.

"David," she said in a soft voice.

David turned to her and looked at her with his dark eyes.

"What have you been drawing in your notebook?" she asked him, seeing if he would just tell her.

He stared at her for a long moment, and then he spoke. "You said we could run. You said it wouldn't follow us. You said it wouldn't find us. You promised."

Stella felt a pang of guilt twist through her. "David, I know I told you that. And I tried." She could feel tears threatening.

David just stared at her.

"I'm sorry," she told him. "I'm doing the best I can."

Finally, he nodded and gave her a small smile.

"When we found you at the dig site, David, you had blood all over you. But you weren't hurt."

David only nodded, staring at her with his dark eyes.

"It wasn't your blood."

He shook his head no slowly.

"Was the blood from your parents?"

David didn't answer; he didn't nod or shake his head no.

"Did that thing out there kill your parents? Did it kill your family?"

David looked away and now Stella could see tears beginning to well up in his eyes. He didn't want to talk about it, she could tell. He didn't want to remember.

She tried a different approach – the notebook, she had to get back to the notebook. "David, what have you been drawing in your notebook?" she asked him again.

He stared at her for a long moment, like he was trying to

decide if he should tell her or not. Finally, he just shook his head no and whispered to her. "I don't know."

"Can I see it?" she asked.

David hesitated; again he seemed unsure of what he should do.

"You can trust me," Stella told David. "You know that. I'm the only one here you can trust."

David nodded and he handed her his notebook.

Stella took the notebook and she smiled at him, trying to give him her warmest smile under the circumstances. "Thank you, David. I just want to take a look."

David nodded and he watched her as she opened the notebook and flipped from one page to the next; she flipped through page after page until she stopped where David had stopped drawing. Nearly two-thirds of the notebook had been filled with David's drawings. She looked at him with shock in her eyes.

"How did you learn how to do this?" she asked him.

David stared at her for a long moment, and then he shook his head no. "I don't know," he told her.

"Do you know what these things are that you've drawn?" she asked him.

"I don't know," he said again.

Maybe he didn't know what was in the notebook, Stella thought, but she knew what it was. And she began to get the first far-off glimpses of hope in her mind. The drawings in this notebook might be the answer, she dared to believe, a way to fight that thing out there.

*

Cole searched through the house for the things they would need while Jose kept and eye and a gun on Needles. Cole could hear Needles pleading with Jose, but Cole knew Jose wouldn't give in. They were all way beyond that now. Maybe they would have time to think about it later, but right now there was something out there that was impossible to fight. And with the sun setting soon, they had no choice but to do what it wanted.

For a few moments Cole was afraid he wouldn't be able to find anything to tie Needles up with and he would have to go out to the garage and look, but then he found a roll of duct tape and a length of rope in the kitchen underneath the cabinets.

Even if he had to go out to the garage, he believed that the thing out there wouldn't kill him as long as he were doing what it wanted.

Maybe, his mind whispered. But how did he know?

What kind of being was out there? What kind of thing could bring the dead back to life? Hollow people out and put pieces of his brother back together and reanimate them, use their bodies like puppets?

Cole didn't want to think about it right now. He needed to concentrate on this task.

But thinking of going out to the garage made him think of the snowmobile for a split second. Did the snowmobile even run? Even though the thing out there had ruined the pickup truck and Stella's Suburban, had it somehow overlooked the snowmobile?

He pushed the thought of the snowmobile from his mind. Maybe this thing could read minds. Who knew how powerful it was? And if it could read minds, then he didn't want to give away his one slim hope of getting away.

Stella had driven away from this thing down in New Mexico (if she was telling the truth, his mind whispered), if she and David had gotten away, then maybe he could too.

Cole placed the tape and the rope on the dining room table and he went into the kitchen to find some tools. There weren't many tools in the cabin; he'd found a hammer, a screwdriver, some nails. He wasn't going out to the garage to look for tools. Instead, he found some spoons and knives in the kitchen drawer, and they would have to do.

A little earlier Cole had searched the cabin for some kind of pain killers, even aspirins, something to help dull the pain for Needles. But there was nothing in the kitchen or the bathroom. He'd found a bottle of Tylenol and a bottle of regular aspirins. But both of the bottles were empty. He wasn't sure if Tom Gordon had left empty bottles behind in his cabinets, or if the bottles had been emptied somehow.

It doesn't want Needles to be anesthetized, his mind whispered. It wants Needles to feel the pain, feel every bit of his eyes being pulled out of his face.

Cole pushed the thought away again as another wave of nausea washed over him.

Cole had wanted to force some whiskey down Needles' throat to help ease the pain, but Jose didn't want to do that; he said it was just a waste of time and they needed to hurry. Cole agreed that they needed to hurry, but he also suspected that Jose wanted to keep the whiskey for himself as a cushion of numbness in case he needed it when the end came.

But Jose was right – they needed to hurry.

Cole and Jose looked at Needles.

It was time.

CHAPTER THIRTY-FIVE

NEEDLES WAS TIED to one of the dining room table chairs with many lengths of rope, duct tape, and two more telephone cords. Jose tied the last of the bonds as Needles struggled and screamed in the chair; the chair's wood creaked from his struggles, and it seemed like it might tip over, but it didn't, and the bonds held.

Jose stood up and backed away from Needles. He glanced at Cole who looked miserable.

"I wish we could've given him something for the pain," Cole muttered.

Jose's expression had turned cold and hard; he was focused on what had to be done. "I told you, we don't have enough time for that. We need to get this done before the sun goes down."

Neither one of them had to look towards the windows in the kitchen or the living room to tell that the sun was setting. The waning afternoon light filtered in through the curtains that covered the window, casting a warm, yellowish light on the gruesome act that they were about to perform.

Needles struggled in his chair, but then he gave up as he breathed heavily – the bonds were too strong, and there were too many of them; there was no hope of him escaping and he realized that now. He looked around, his eyes wild with panic. He glanced at Jose, but he knew that there was no bargaining with Jose, his only chance would be with Cole.

"You're making a big mistake, Cole" Needles said, trying

to keep his voice as calm and reasonable-sounding as possible. "That kid, he's doing all of this somehow. I know it."

Cole looked away.

"Listen to me, please. You need to kill that kid. That kid's doing all of this. He's the demon. The devil. He's going to get all of you in the end if you don't kill him first."

Jose stood by the table and inspected the "tools" that Cole had laid out: various spoons, a few different kinds of kitchen knives, a bowl, some rags for cleaning up. The duct tape was near the tools. He picked up the roll of duct tape and tossed it to Cole. "Shut him up, will you?"

Cole caught the roll of tape.

Needles' eyes followed the tape and he stared at Cole, pleading with him. "No, wait! You have to listen to me! I'm not crazy! I know what's going on here! It's that kid!"

Cole wrapped the duct tape around Needles' mouth, wrapping it around his head several times, covering the lower half of his face with the tape.

Needles screamed into the tape and struggled again. Tears flowed from his eyes as he sobbed into the tape.

Jose picked up a small, serrated kitchen knife and stood in front of Needles. He looked at Cole who stood behind Needles. "You ready?" he asked Cole.

Cole managed a small nod as he swallowed hard. "I guess."

"Hold him still," Jose said.

Cole grabbed each side of Needles' head and held him as still as he could. He pried Needles' left eyelid open with his fingers as he held him.

Jose brought the tip of the knife close to Needles' left eye which was bulging with fear, the eye couldn't look away, couldn't help but watch the tip of the knife as it got closer and closer, the knife shook a little in Jose's unsteady hand.

Just as Jose was about to sink the tip of the blade into the side of Needles' eyeball, Needles moved and Jose jabbed Needles in the cheek just below the eye; the wound began to bleed immediately, the blood ran down his cheek and down the tape, the blood dripped down onto the cross hanging outside of his thermal shirt.

Jose backed away, suddenly angry. "Shit, man. You've got to hold him still."

Cole dropped his hands away from Needles' head and backed away. "I'm trying. He's struggling too much."

Jose sighed and set the knife back on the table. He pulled his gun out from the waistband of his pants and he walked around to the back of Needles.

"Struggling too much?" Jose asked, and then he wacked Needles on the back of the head with the butt of his gun, knocking Needles out instantly.

Needles' head slumped forward and his breathing was even and steady out of his nose.

Jose stuffed his gun back into his pants and walked back to the table. He picked up the knife and a spoon. He looked at Cole. "Hold his eyelids open. I'm sure it doesn't want these eyeballs damaged."

Cole shuddered, but he moved in beside Jose. He pried Needles' left eye open and the eyeball stared back at them, lifeless and unconscious.

"I'm going to cut it out and you get the bowl ready to put it in."

"Just hurry," Cole said.

*

Thirty minutes later, Cole and Jose sat at the dining room table, both of them exhausted. Needles was still unconscious and tied to the dining room table chair, his bloody head hung forward, blood-stained gauze and duct tape were wrapped around his face where his eyes used to be, but the tape was off of his mouth now to allow him to breathe more easily.

Stella and David were still in the bedroom. Cole was about

to go and get them. He and Jose had cleaned up the mess around Needles as best as they could. They put his eyeballs in a bowl and left them out on the front porch – a gift for that monster out there.

Suddenly, Needles woke up. He lifted his head up and screamed. "My eyes! You took my eyes!"

Cole jumped to his feet and ran over to Needles. "Just try to calm down, Needles." His own words sounded surreal to his ears, this whole situation seemed unreal to him.

"It hurts!" Needles howled. "It hurts so bad! Why did you do this to me, Cole?"

"You deserved it, you sick son of a bitch," Jose said; he was still seated at the dining room table, a few feet away from Needles. "If you hadn't shot that old man in the bank, we wouldn't even be here."

Needles wouldn't stop crying and screaming. "Oh, God, where are you, Cole?" Needles rocked his head back and forth like he was trying to look around the room with eyes he didn't have anymore.

"I'm right here," Cole said from right beside Needles. Tears brimmed in his eyes as he looked at Needles, once his friend, now tied to a chair with his eyes carved out. What had he done? Cole asked himself. What had he become?

Needles still looked around as he moaned, like he couldn't quite place where Cole was. "It hurts so bad!! I can't take the pain!"

"Shut the fuck up!" Jose screamed at Needles, and then he got to his feet beside the table and glanced at Cole. "Shut him up again, please." Jose paced away from the table, into the hallway, he needed to be away from Needles, he couldn't take the crying anymore, but even in here he could still hear Needles screaming and moaning.

"Please, Cole. I can't take the pain anymore. I ... I can't take – "

Needles' last words were cut off by a booming gunshot in the cabin.

Jose rushed back out from the hallway to see Cole standing behind Needles; Cole had his gun in his hand, still aimed at the back of Needles' head. Needles was slumped forward in the chair as far as the rope and tape would allow him. His head was pitched forward and blood drained from the large wound in his forehead where the bullet had exploded out of his face. The gauze and tape over his eyes was stained dark red already, and a puddle of blood was forming on the floor in front of the chair.

Jose stared at Cole in shock. "What the fuck did you do?"

Cole shook his head no as he stared at Jose with a vacant look in his eyes. "I couldn't leave him suffering like that. I couldn't let him keep feeling that kind of pain."

Jose paced around the living room, a rage building in him quickly. He ran his hand through his dark hair several times. "Did you stop to think that the thing outside didn't want him dead?"

Cole watched Jose. "I don't care. I wasn't going to let him keep on suffering."

Jose punched his fist at the air a few times in frustration, and then he turned to Cole. "Fuck! We needed Needles! What are we supposed to do if that thing out there wants another body part? We could've used Needles over and over again."

Cole felt that now familiar wave of nausea washing over him again, but this time it was Jose that nauseated him. He could feel his own rage building up inside of him, that rage that had been just beneath the surface of him the whole time he'd been in this cabin. "Let's get Needles out on the front porch, and then it can have all the body parts it wants."

CHAPTER THIRTY-SIX

AS THE SUN dipped down below the forest of trees in the west and the winter sky darkened in the east, Needles' body lay on the floorboards of the front porch not too far away from his eyeballs which were offered up in one of Tom Gordon's plastic cereal bowls. Both eyeballs faced the woods like they were looking at them. The freezing wind had picked up a little and the trees swayed, but there wasn't any snow falling yet.

Inside the cabin Cole, Jose, and Stella sat at the dining room table. The area in the dining room had been cleaned up as much as possible, but the chair that Needles had been tied to was still stained with blood and it was pushed in at the table, the back facing the hallway. The wood floor still had dark smears of blood stained into it from where Cole and Jose had dragged Needles' body outside. The coils of bloody rope and telephone cords were piled up near the freezer, and the duct tape and gauze that had been wrapped around Needles' head and body was now in the trash can.

David sat on the couch and watched the three as they sat at the table. He had his spiral notebook near him, but he wasn't drawing in it now – it seemed like he was done with the things he had drawn. Every few minutes David glanced at the front door like he was expecting someone to come to the door.

Jose sat at the table with his hands curled around the whiskey bottle. He sipped from the bottle every few minutes and he was beginning to get a little drunk. He was beginning to lose his control just a little. But he didn't care; he needed the numbness that the whiskey brought with it, even if just for a little while.

Cole and Stella sat close to each other at the table. The cabin was silent; the only sound that could be heard was the whistling winter wind outside playing around the eaves. In the silence, Stella spoke.

"I'm an archeologist," she said, and then she looked at Cole.

Cole nodded; she'd already told him that before. He was tired now, beyond exhaustion. He wasn't sure how many nights he'd stayed awake, and he was pretty sure he'd had only about eight hours of sleep in the last few days.

"I specialize in the cultures of the Southwest Native Americans," Stella continued, and it seemed like she was leading somewhere this time, like there was something she finally wanted to tell them, something she finally wanted to reveal. "Especially the Anasazi. The Anasazi were a group of people who lived in that region hundreds of years ago. They built massive cities all over the region. They built kivas and they constructed roads that went on for miles and miles. They built some of their cities right into the sides of cliffs, massive cities carved right into the solid rock. The only way to get up to the city was by ladders or hand and toe holds carved right into the rock."

Stella sipped her coffee. She glanced at David who watched her, and then she looked at Cole who was listening to her. "These cities, and some of their other cities, were highly defensible, like they were constantly at war and constantly defending them-selves, like they were constantly afraid of something. Some sci-entists speculate that they were afraid of other tribes of Indians. But at that time, the Anasazi were the most advanced tribe in that area, maybe even in all of North America. Who would they need to be afraid of?"

Jose sipped his bottle of whiskey. "Is this going somewhere?" he asked her, his words slurring just slightly.

"About seven hundred years ago the Anasazi vanished," Stella continued, undaunted by Jose's remark.

"Like many groups of people in North and South America, the Anasazi built massive cities and roads, they built an entire civilization, and then they abandoned them, like they just walked away. Recent findings at some Anasazi sites have uncovered mass graves of murder victims and evidence of cannibalism."

"The history lesson is fascinating …" Jose said and let his words trail off as he sipped more whiskey.

Stella ignored Jose as she went on. "I got a call from a colleague, a man named Jake. He told me that he'd made an amazing discovery, the greatest of his life. Maybe one of the most amazing and important discoveries in archeological history, and he asked for my help. He needed my expertise of the Anasazi history."

Stella paused for a moment, sipped more coffee, and then she continued. "Jake wanted everything kept quiet until we were sure what we'd really found. I drove there and met him at the dig site. It was amazing. Jake had found a hidden cave system, and inside the cave were the ruins of a civilization. An Anasazi civilization, I was sure of it."

Cole stared at Stella. "And that's where this happened to you and David. Like what's happening here."

"Yes. That's where I found David. He was bloody, but not hurt. But he couldn't remember what had happened. He wouldn't even talk to any of us at first. He was afraid of everyone. Except me."

Stella looked at David to gauge his reaction. He just stared back at her with his dark eyes, eyes that were almost black. He sat motionless on the couch, not moving a muscle.

"Not long after we found David, that's when everything started to go wrong. Jake suggested that one of us take David to the nearest Navajo village and get some help for him. But …" Stella glanced at David again.

David watched her and then he looked at the front door.

"But our vehicles wouldn't start. There was nothing wrong with them, they just wouldn't start. Like all of the batteries had died at the same time."

David's breathing grew quicker as he watched the door.

"Then the first person went missing. Jim Whitefeather, a friend of mine. He left in the middle of the night like he just walked off into the desert. Or into the cave."

"But then he came back," Cole finished for her.

Stella nodded.

"What did he ask for?" Cole asked.

"It was like this. He asked for body parts."

"And you guys gave him what he asked for?"

"Not at first," Stella answered quickly. "We tried to run. Tried to escape. Tried to fight back. But it wouldn't let us go. It made an example out of one of us."

Cole stared at her.

"An example like Trevor," she explained.

Cole flinched at his brother's name. Cole looked away, thinking for a moment as he pushed the thought of his brother out of his mind. Then he looked back at Stella as a thought occurred to him. "So this thing just took you guys one by one, and then asked for body parts? And you don't know why."

"It was making us do things. Trying to scare us so badly that we'd do anything it wanted, anything it asked us to do no matter what it was."

"Because it was leading up to something," Cole said.

Stella saw a movement out of the corner of her eye. She glanced over at David and saw that he was frightened now as he stared at the front door. He was up on his feet, standing next to the couch. She looked back at Cole as he asked his next question.

"It was leading up to something specific," Cole told her. "Wasn't it?"

Stella didn't answer. Cole had figured it out. A quick glance at Jose told her that Jose was getting drunk now and not really listening to them anymore, his eyes were nearly closed, pure exhaustion taking over his body.

"It's leading up to something specific here, too," Cole said, staring at her with an expression that seemed accusatory and victorious at the same time. "You know what it wants, don't you?" he asked, his voice getting louder. It was even beginning to rouse Jose from his drunken slumber.

Stella looked over at David. He took a step towards the front door, then another, almost like he was in a trance.

Cole turned in his chair and looked at David, and then he turned back and looked at Stella. "You know what it's going to ask for next," he said even louder. "You know what it wants."

"He's out there," David said from the living room.

This brought Jose fully awake. He jumped up from his chair and spun around on his feet and stared at David. Then he looked at Cole and Stella, the fear was back in his eyes now.

David took another two steps towards the door, and then he stopped and looked at Cole. "He's calling you."

CHAPTER THIRTY-SEVEN

JOSE DIDN'T WASTE any time. He grabbed his coat and walked right to the front door on legs that were a little unsteady from the amount of whiskey he'd drank in a short amount of time.

"Jose, wait," Cole said a low voice.

Jose turned and looked at Cole through red-rimmed and terrified eyes. "No, we need to go out there. We can't keep it waiting. We have to do whatever it wants."

Jose turned and marched towards the front door.

Cole and Stella exchanged glances. Stella nodded and Cole followed Jose to the door. Jose was already unlocking the deadbolt. Stella took David's hand and they both followed Cole and Jose outside onto the porch.

The four gathered outside on the porch, a few steps away from the door. Stella was closest to the door. She closed the door almost all the way, leaving it open just a crack. The yellowish light from inside the cabin could be seen through the crack in the doorway. Outside, the world was growing dark very quickly. And it was getting colder.

Frank stood in the same spot as he had before, only thirty yards away from the cabin. The snow was up to his calves and he wore the same clothes. He stood very still, no movement at all, almost just a shadow himself in the pitch black darkness that was descending on the land as the night moved in.

Cole stared at Frank, and he thought of what Jose had said, about Frank's body being hollowed out. Yet here he stood. Cole believed Jose now after seeing his own brother's pieces put back together into a walking and talking body.

Frank stared at them with a blank expression; there were no fake smiles from him anymore, no need to pretend any longer. They knew Frank was just a hollowed-out corpse now, just a meat puppet with some all-powerful, invisible force pulling his strings. Frank spoke in a loud, guttural voice. "He is very pleased so far. He believes you are ready for your final task."

The four waited on the porch. None of them moved or said anything. They didn't shout back at Frank like they had done before; they didn't challenge him, or threaten him. What else could they do but listen to his demand?

"When you give him this one last thing he wants," Frank continued, "then he will let you walk out of here untouched. You will be allowed to keep your money and leave."

They were silent for a long moment, and then Cole finally spoke up. "What does he want?"

Stella held her breath. Cole had been right earlier in the cabin; she did know what Frank was going to ask for next. She knew all along what this was leading up to – one final task, one final request from this thing. She looked at David. She still held his hand, and she squeezed his hand a little harder.

David knew it, too.

They braced themselves as Frank answered Cole.

"He wants you to kill the boy."

They were all silent, not sure how to react. Cole and Jose both looked behind them at Stella and David. It was just a brief glance from both of them, but Frank's voice turned them back around.

"Kill the boy and leave his body on the front porch. Then all of this will be over."

Cole shook his head no. This was too much. He had helped carve out his friend's eyeballs earlier today, and this was going way too far now. How much more could he do? Where was the line? He couldn't kill a little kid.

"No," Cole said loudly as his breath plumed up in front of his mouth from the cold.

No reaction yet from Jose, Stella, or David.

No reaction from Frank.

"We can't do that!" Cole yelled out to Frank.

Frank still didn't answer. He began to glide back towards the trees, his legs didn't move, it was like some invisible string was pulling him back to the dark mass of trees, or like he was on some kind of conveyer belt hidden underneath the snow. But he wasn't answering Cole. He wasn't arguing with Cole. He wasn't threatening Cole. He didn't need to. It didn't need to. They all knew what it could do.

"We can't do that!!" Cole yelled louder, and he stepped to the edge of the porch.

Jose stepped away from Cole and turned around and looked at Stella and David, keeping an eye on them as they stood near the front door. He spoke to Cole, but he kept his eyes on Stella and David, making sure that they weren't going to dart back inside and try to lock them out here. "Cole, listen to me for a second."

Cole turned and looked at Jose. "Jose, no ..."

"Just think about it for a second," Jose continued in a very calm tone, his voice soft and reasonable. "It's asking for one life to spare the rest of us. One life for three, and then we can leave."

"You think that thing's going to let us leave?" Cole asked Jose.

"It doesn't matter!" Jose snapped. His reasonable voice was suddenly gone now. "We have to do what it wants! I'm not going to end up like Frank. Or Trevor!"

Hearing his brother's name stung Cole for a moment, he looked away, his defenses down and Jose pulled out his pistol from his coat pocket and aimed it at Cole, but his eyes kept darting back to Stella and David.

"What the fuck are you doing?" Cole asked Jose.

"Stay right there," Jose warned. He looked at Stella and David. "You two don't move."

"Let's think about this, Jose," Cole begged.

"Put your hands up," Jose told Cole.

"Jose, we can't do this."

"We'll just put a bullet in that kid's head," Jose said. "That's all. He'll never feel a thing. He'll never see it coming."

"We can't do that."

Jose held his gun steady on Cole even though he'd drank a lot of whiskey earlier. His eyes kept darting back to Stella and David. But then he looked at Cole when he said his next words.

"You might as well tell Stella the truth," Jose told Cole.

CHAPTER THIRTY-EIGHT

"TELL HER THE truth!" Jose repeated to Cole.

"What the hell are you talking about?"

Stella watched Cole and Jose. She was ready to bolt inside with David, but she couldn't take a chance on Jose shooting at them; they'd never make it inside – she had to wait for the right time.

"Jose, why don't you put the gun down?" Cole said. "We can discuss this."

"There's nothing to discuss!" Jose spat out. He looked at Stella and David. "We were going to kill you two anyway," Jose said. "That's the truth. We couldn't leave two witnesses alive."

"That's a lie!" Cole said. "We never discussed anything like that."

"Nobody discussed anything with *you*, Cole. You weren't part of the team anymore. You just did this job to help your brother, to get him out of debt with Frank. Nobody trusted you anymore. Me and Frank didn't trust either one of you anymore."

"That's a fucking lie!" Cole said, but there wasn't as much force in his words now. He was beginning to see what may have really been going on. Frank and Jose were discussing things behind their backs. Were they going to kill him and Trevor after they killed Stella and David? Split the money up between the three of them? Or maybe they were going to kill Needles, too. There was a lot of money at stake this time, and perhaps they had been ready to kill for it.

Jose looked at Stella again, and he gave her his best smile, what he thought was his most reassuring smile in the near darkness. "But listen, Stella," he said. He was calling her by her name now. "We don't have to kill you now. We just have to kill David."

"We're not killing that kid," Cole said. "We have to think of another way." Cole's mind was spinning as he realized that Frank and Jose had been planning on killing everyone involved.

"There is no other way!" Jose snapped.

Cole noticed Jose's body swaying just a bit, just a little unsteady on his feet. His hand holding the gun was beginning to tremble. This is my only chance, Cole thought. Jose isn't going to wait much longer out here in the cold before he shoots David. Or all three of us.

"Just listen to me for a second, Jose," Cole said, trying to stall for time, trying to wait for exactly the right time to charge.

Jose was about to explode with rage again – he was only a few seconds away from shooting, Cole was sure of that. But then Jose's attention was distracted for a second by David opening the front door of the cabin.

Jose turned his gun on David.

Stella stepped in front of David, ready to take a bullet for him.

But Jose didn't care – he'd shoot through Stella to get to that kid if he had to.

Stella squeezed her eyes shut.

This was Cole's only chance. He rushed at Jose and tackled him just as Jose's finger pulled the trigger. The gun fired, but Cole had knocked Jose's arm away just enough and the bullet whizzed past Stella and struck the cabin wall.

Cole slammed Jose into the side of the cabin, and he heard a grunt as the breath left Jose's lungs for a moment.

"Get inside!" Cole yelled at Stella and David.

Stella grabbed David and pushed at him to get inside, but David was already a step ahead of her. They hurried inside and slammed the door shut. Stella looked down at the door handle.

She looked at the lock on the door handle. At the deadbolt. She couldn't take a chance. She locked the door.

Outside on the porch, Cole and Jose wrestled. Cole had a grip on Jose's wrist, keeping the gun pointed down at the floorboards of the front porch. They wrestled on their feet for a moment, but with one violent twist of his body, Cole swung Jose over him in a Judo flip and they both landed on the floorboards of the front porch with Cole on top of Jose.

The gun went off.

The shot was loud in the eerie silence of the dark night all around the cabin. It echoed across the snowy fields.

Inside the cabin, Stella and David watched the door. They had heard the gunshot. Who was shot? Was it Cole? Jose? Both of them?

*

Cole got up off of Jose and his hands went to his own abdomen, afraid he'd been shot and didn't feel it yet. But his bare hands came away dry. No blood on him. He looked down at Jose who wasn't moving. Even in the darkness, Cole could see the darker stain spreading across Jose's shirt underneath his open coat. Cole didn't even remember shooting; he wasn't even sure how it had happened.

It had happened so fast.

Cole picked up Jose's gun from the porch and he aimed it down at Jose.

Jose stared up at Cole with wide eyes, he was afraid, he knew what had happened. He opened his mouth to speak and he coughed up a chunk of pulpy blood and then gasped for air.

Cole backed away from Jose, he moved closer to the front door of the cabin.

Jose's body trembled as he sat up and scooted across the floorboards to the log wall of the cabin. He pushed himself up into a sitting position with his back against the cabin wall. He gritted his teeth and moaned in pain; his hands shot to his abdomen, holding on to it, trying in vain to stop the flow of blood.

Cole turned and looked out at the snowy field. "We left you a bonus!!" he screamed out at the woods. Then he turned to walk to the front door and Jose's hand grabbed Cole's pants leg, stopping him for a second.

Jose stared up at Cole with wide, terrified eyes. "Please, Cole. Don't leave me out here for that thing."

Cole stared down at Jose for a moment, and then he ripped his pants leg out of Jose's grasp and he walked to the front door of the cabin. He twisted the door handle but it wouldn't open – it was locked.

He beat on the door. "Let me in!" He screamed at the door. "Stella, it's me, Cole! Jose is shot! He's not coming inside with me!"

No answer from inside.

Cole could hear Jose chuckling from the darkness. That chuckle turned into a laugh. "Now who's been double crossed?"

"Shut the fuck up," Cole said.

"We'll just both have to wait out here now," Jose said. "We'll both have to see what comes for us out of the darkness."

There was a sound from the dark woods at the edge of the snowy field, a loud sound, like something very big was crashing through the trees. Cole turned and stared at the darkness, nearly all the light from the setting sun was gone now, and the world around them was blanketed in almost pure darkness. And there was something in the woods, coming closer.

Cole turned back to the door and pounded on it. "Let me in! There's something in the woods, I can hear it!"

CHAPTER THIRTY-NINE

STELLA AND DAVID stared at the front door. They could hear Cole beating on the door and demanding to be let in. Cole said it was only him and that Jose had been shot. But could she believe him?

David touched Stella's hand. He nodded his head yes.

Stella nodded back at David, and she took a deep breath. She moved close to the door and talked through it. "It's only you, Cole?" she asked.

"Yes," Cole answered, and there was panic in his voice. "You have to hurry. I can hear something out in the trees. It's something big."

Stella looked back at David one more time, making sure. Then she opened the door and Cole rushed inside.

Stella closed and locked the door. She twisted the knob for the deadbolt. Then she backed away from the door and stared at Cole.

Cole stood only a few feet away from Stella, closer to the kitchen. He looked very cold even though he was only outside for a few minutes, but he didn't have his coat, hat, or gloves. He stood very still and stared at her.

Stella began to wonder if she'd made the wrong decision letting him in.

"You were going to leave me out there?" Cole asked Stella in a strangely calm voice. "Leave me out there in the cold? Out there with that thing?"

"I ... I had to be sure," she told him.

"I just killed another friend of mine to save you and David. How is that not enough?"

"You've seen now what that thing can do," Stella answered quickly, a sudden anger in her voice. "I had to be sure it was really you."

Cole walked away from Stella and let out a long breath. He inhaled deeply, trying to calm himself down, trying to think rationally. But he'd been through so much in the last few days, seen things he never thought were possible, hadn't had much sleep or food, and now thinking rationally was a little more difficult than it used to be.

He grabbed the bottle of whiskey and took a sip, letting the fiery liquid relax him a little. He turned and looked at Stella who stood in the same spot in the living room, staring at him. He had frightened her, but at least she was trying to trust him.

She had trusted him enough to let him back inside, and he needed to trust her. "This is what it's been leading up to the whole time, isn't it?" he asked Stella.

She nodded yes.

"This is the same thing that it led up to at the dig site, isn't it?"

Stella glanced at David, and then she looked back at Cole. She sighed heavily and nodded. "Yes."

"Why does it want us to kill David? He's just a kid. Why doesn't it just come in here and do it?"

Stella hesitated for a moment, staring at Cole. "I don't think it can," she finally answered him. "I think it's afraid of David for some reason. I don't think it's able to kill David so it needs others to do it. It tries to scare others so badly that they will do anything it wants – even kill a little boy."

There was a pounding on the front door.

They all jumped.

From the other side of the door, they heard Jose's voice. "Cole, let me in! I'm not dead yet!"

They all stood very still and stared at the door.

"I need help," Jose continued from out on the porch. He beat on the door again. "Please, I'm bleeding bad, man. Please don't leave me out here!" They could hear that Jose was beginning to cry. "Please don't leave me out here with this thing!"

Cole took a step towards the door; he rested his hand on top of the butt of his gun that stuck up from the waistband of his pants.

"I won't hurt David," Jose said from behind the door. "I promise. Just let me in."

Cole took another step closer to the door, he stared at it. It couldn't be Jose, Cole thought to himself. Jose had to be dead by now. Or taken by that thing out there.

"We'll think of another way," Jose said from the other side of the door. "Like you said, we'll think of something else. We won't kill David."

As Cole stared at the door, he took another step towards it. David jumped off the couch and ran across the floor to Cole. He grabbed Cole's hand and took it in his own hand, like a son would grab his father's hand. Cole looked down at David who stared up at him.

"It's not him anymore," David told Cole in a soft voice.

Cole nodded down at David. "I know," he told him.

There was a sudden flurry of poundings on the door. Jose screamed at them from the other side of the door, and his voice was no longer pleading; now it was angry. "You're going to be very sorry, Cole! It will get you just like it got me! It won't let you die. You just go on and on. Just like Frank! Just like Trevor!"

Jose's voice turned deeper as he continued shouting, his voice became more guttural, more demonic. "Kill the boy, or it's going to be bad. So bad. Worse than you can possibly imagine!"

There was a rush of wind from outside and the door shook and rattled in its frame.

And then everything was deathly quiet.

Cole looked down at David who still held his hand and stared up at him with his dark eyes.

Cole knelt down and got on the same eye level as David. "Don't worry, David. We're not going to hurt you. We're not going to give you to that thing outside. We'll find a way out of here. I promise."

David stared at Cole for a moment, then he jumped at Cole and hugged him, squeezing him tightly, his eyes shut, a few tears slipping out of his eyes.

Cole was a little shocked by David's sudden hug. He glanced over at Stella who watched them. She wiped away a stray tear from her eye.

David let Cole go and he ran back to the couch.

Cole got back up to his feet and he looked at Stella. "We have to try and run," he told her.

Stella just stared at him.

"But we can't run at night," Cole went on. "We need to get through this night and leave in the morning." Cole pulled Jose's gun out of the waistband of his pants from under the back of his shirt. He held it by the barrel and walked over to Stella. He handed it to her.

Stella took Jose's gun.

"Do you know how to use one of these?" Cole asked her.

Stella looked down at the gun in her hand, and then in a blur of motion, she expertly checked the clip for bullets, then popped the clip back in. She racked a bullet into the chamber, and then checked to make sure the safety was on.

Cole stared at her in amazement.

Stella gave Cole a small smile. "I taught myself how to use guns a few years ago. A girl by herself at remote dig sites can be a little unnerving."

Cole smiled. "You're full of surprises."

He looked at the front door. "Since we're going to be stuck here for the night, I think it's a good idea to barricade the front door and windows."

CHAPTER FORTY

THE NIGHT WAS eerily quiet and calm. There was no winter wind whistling in the eaves around the cabin. There were no sounds of Frank or Jose calling out to them from out in the snow. No sounds of footsteps on the front porch. Everything was just … quiet.

Earlier in the night Cole barricaded the front windows and doors as best as he could. He managed to tear apart the dining room table and chairs so he could use the wood for the barricades. He used the hammer and various nails he'd found earlier in the cabinet underneath the sink. He used slats from underneath the beds and nailed the pieces of wood over the back door and the windows that looked out onto the front porch. They shoved Needles' recliner against the front door; it wasn't much of a barricade, but they didn't want to use the couch as a barricade because none of them wanted to sit in the chair that Needles had occupied for so much of the time he was in the cabin. They upended the dining room table and shoved it against the entrance to the hallway. It closed off the bathroom to them, but they would just have to make do.

None of them wanted to go into the bathroom anyway after what happened to Trevor.

It was late, nearly two o'clock in the morning. David fell asleep on the couch. Cole and Stella sat on the floor in front of the couch, like they were guarding David.

Stella had Jose's gun beside her on the floor. She stifled a yawn, trying to stay awake.

Cole looked at her. "I just wanted you to know that this was supposed to be my last bank job."

Stella stared at him for a moment. "You guys seemed like an experienced group."

"I used to be a part of Frank's crew. Then I quit. But then Trevor got involved with them. He ended up owing Frank some money – a lot of money – and I needed to help them with one last job to help Trevor pay him back."

Stella nodded.

"I don't expect you to believe me; I just wanted to tell you that this was going to be my last time." Cole thought for a moment. "I was really trying to change. I just wished I would've changed a little sooner. Before I got Trevor involved …"

"I'm sorry," Stella said in a soft voice. "I'm an only child. I can't imagine what it must feel like to lose a brother."

They were both quiet for a long moment in the murky cabin. They had turned all the lights off except for the light over the stove.

"How did you get away from that dig site in New Mexico?" Cole asked Stella.

Stella looked at Cole, trying to determine if there was any accusation in his eyes or in the tone of his voice.

"You said your vehicles wouldn't start," Cole continued. "And then you said that the thing out there was taking your friends one by one."

Stella sighed. "Even before I realized that the thing out there wanted David, I began to suspect that there was something … something special about David." Stella stole a quick glance at David – he was still sleeping peacefully. "When the thing asked the few of us who remained to kill David, I began to believe that it needed us to kill David because it couldn't do it by itself."

"So David is …" Cole thought for a moment, trying to find the right words. "He's special. Like powerful. Like you think he has powers?"

"There were only a few of us left," Stella said in a low voice, looking away from Cole. "And Jake, my friend, he hadn't been taken yet. But Jake and the others wanted to kill David. They felt like it was their only way out. I tried to convince them that once we gave it what it wanted, it wouldn't let us go. It would just kill all of us because it wouldn't need us anymore. But I couldn't convince them, they had their minds made up, they wanted to kill David. So I took him and I ran to my truck."

"And you knew it would start?"

"Yeah, I had a feeling it would," Stella answered him. "It was a big gamble, but it was the only choice I had left." Stella didn't mention to Cole that she had watched Jake slit his own throat rather than let that thing take him alive.

They were quiet for a moment.

Stella thought of the things David had drawn in his book. She needed to take another chance right now, she needed to trust Cole. "I want to show you something else," she said. "I want to trust you. And I want you to trust me even though I know you don't have any reason to since I've hidden so much until now …"

"You had to," Cole said quickly. "I understand why you did it." Cole thought of her trusting him, and then he thought of the secret he'd kept to himself all this time – the snowmobile in the garage. But who knew if it would even work. The snowmobile could be old or damaged. Or maybe that thing out there knew it was there. Maybe that thing could read minds and had learned of the snowmobile from Cole's thoughts.

Cole pushed the thought of the snowmobile out of his mind as Stella turned and carefully pulled the spiral notebook out from under David. She opened the notebook and showed Cole what was inside.

He took the notebook and flipped through page after page of what looked like some kind of symbols. He wasn't sure what he was looking at, but it seemed like some kind of ancient language.

He looked at her, not really understanding what he was looking at.

"It's the Anasazi language," she told him in an awed voice.

Cole shook his head a little. "David's been writing in this language?" Cole shrugged his shoulders like it shouldn't be a big deal. "Isn't David Native American?"

"Yes. I'm pretty sure he's Navajo; most likely full-blooded. But he's never told me much about himself."

"But this Ana … ana …"

"Anasazi. Like I told you before, they lived hundreds of years ago and then they vanished. No one knows where they went to. Some say they intermingled with other tribes, or even became other tribes. Some say they left the area. Others even speculated that the Anasazi were the remnants of the Maya who also built massive cities and then abandoned them. But no one knows for sure."

Cole nodded his head.

"The Anasazi, like many ancient peoples of North and South America, had no written language, or at least no significant evidence had ever been found."

It was beginning to sink in a little to Cole.

"There have been bits and pieces of Anasazi symbols found, but not much, not enough to get a clear overview of any kind of language. It's sort of like Egyptian hieroglyphics."

Cole nodded; he'd heard of Egyptian hieroglyphics before.

"I asked David how he learned how to write all of this, but he said he didn't know."

Cole glanced down at the notebook which was filled with page after page of symbols. All this time in the cabin David had been scribbling down these symbols, one after the other. He looked at Stella. "Can you read it?"

"I can recognize some of the symbols, enough to know that it's from the Anasazi culture, but I can't make enough of it out to understand any of it."

Cole sighed, thinking this over. "So David definitely has something to do with all of this. He has some kind of powers, he knows about that thing out there."

Stella sat up a little, becoming a little excited, her eyes lit up a little in the darkness of the cabin. "The word Anasazi is a Navajo word," she continued. "A lot of times the word is translated as Ancient Ones. But a more accurate translation is Ancient Enemy."

"So the Navajo called this tribe their ancient enemies?" Cole asked.

"That's what most scholars believe. But I have a different theory."

Cole waited for Stella to continue. He could tell that she was a little excited, archeology was definitely her passion.

"I believe that Anasazi wasn't a word that the Navajo used to name the tribe, I believe it's a word they used to describe the beings that took the Anasazi and caused them to vanish."

CHAPTER FORTY-ONE

"LIKE I TOLD you before," Stella went on, "the Anasazi were a very advanced culture at that time, about seven to eight hundred years ago; they were the most advanced culture in North America. They had no one to fear, yet they built these massive cities right into the sides of cliffs. Why go through all of that work if they were the strongest and most advanced tribe?"

Cole didn't answer. He knew he couldn't keep up with Stella on this level of conversation. He just let her continue.

"All these years archeologists have always wondered what they were defending themselves from. What were they so afraid of? And after all of that work, what would make them suddenly leave these cities? Or the Maya. Or the Olmecs. Or the Inca. Something drove them out of their cities. Some say it was because of drought or shortage of food supplies, but other tribes stayed in the same regions."

Stella took a breath; she had been talking so fast, her voice getting louder. She glanced at David to make sure she hadn't disturbed him. "There are many legends in Native American cultures about demons that would come in the night and take people. Sometimes these demons would ask for things, offerings. And if these offerings weren't given to them, then they would take people. And supposedly the only people who could see these demons were the shamans. Like witch doctors."

Cole nodded to indicate that he understood what a shaman was.

"What if David can see that thing out there? What if the

reason it wants to kill David is because he's a shaman – natural-born shaman?"

Cole just stared at her.

"Many believe that shamans were people who may have been born with some kind of psychic or telekinetic abilities. And they used these … these skills to wield power over their tribe."

"So you think David is a natural shaman? You think he's psychic or telekinetic?"

"I think he might be, even though he doesn't know it yet."

Stella looked at the front door with the recliner in front of it. She looked back at Cole.

"I don't know what that thing is out there. A demon? I don't know. The Native American legends of demons predate Christianity. An alien? Who knows? There are many theories of visitations by aliens to cultures in North, Central, and South America. The Nazca Plains. The Hopi Indian rituals. The sacrifices at the temples in the Maya culture may have not been religious ceremonies to their gods. What if they were offerings to that thing out there through the years? Maybe that thing out there only comes around every few hundred years. What if a day to it is a hundred years to us, and a night of sleeping to it is a hundred years?" Stella had been talking so fast, she stopped and stared into Cole's eyes where she could see doubt and confusion.

"So you think that thing out there might be an alien? Like from outer space? Like from a UFO?"

"Maybe they've been here for a long, long time," she said quickly. "Even before human civilization. I know it sounds far-fetched, but look around you. You've seen what that thing can do."

Cole only nodded.

"I think that thing out there may roam the Earth, unseen and unfelt by most. But then every once in a while someone like David comes along; someone who can see it, feel it, maybe even fight it."

Suddenly, Cole became a little excited. He could see a glimmer of hope, a small dot of light at the end of this long horrible tunnel they were in. "So you're saying that we can get David to kill this thing?"

"I don't know if it's that easy."

"What do you mean?"

"David may be a natural-born shaman, but he's still just a boy. He's had no training. He may not even know what to do."

"Great," Cole said and sighed. "Then I guess we're back to square one. We try and run in the morning."

"It may be all we can do for now," Stella told him. "But we need to protect David. That's the most important thing."

Cole leaned back against the couch and let out another long sigh. He looked at Stella who yawned again. "Why don't you get an hour's rest? I know you need it. I'll stand guard for a little while."

Stella nodded. "I'll try. Wake me up if you hear anything."

"I will. Just try and get some rest. Tomorrow morning may be very stressful."

*

Almost three hours later everything was still quiet outside. Cole hadn't heard a single sound from out there, not even the wind.

He sat near the kitchen in the only dining room chair that they hadn't broken apart and used as wood for the barricades over the windows. He watched Stella and David. Both of them were asleep, both of them breathing heavily.

Cole watched them for a while. He needed to make sure they were asleep.

He got to his feet, being as quiet as he could.

He looked at the clock on the kitchen wall. It would be dawn very soon.

He knew what he needed to do now.

CHAPTER FORTY-TWO

COLE OPENED THE refrigerator. He had rummaged around in here for some food earlier. They had eaten a lot of it so far. But he had seen something earlier that he thought he could use – a can of soda in the bottom drawer underneath a head of wilted lettuce. He took out the can of soda from the crisper drawer and set it on the counter next to the stove. It was a cheap brand of cola. But it didn't matter to him because he wasn't going to drink it.

He peeked into the living room.

Stella and David were both still asleep.

Cole looked back at the stove. It was a gas stove. He lifted up the top and blew out the pilot light. He lowered the lid carefully, trying not to make a sound. Once the lid was back down, he turned on all of the burners and the oven. He could already smell the rotten egg smell of gas coming out of the burners.

He grabbed the can of soda from the counter and shook it up. Then he opened the microwave oven and set the can inside. He closed the door and set the timer on the microwave for thirty minutes. The digital numbers began counting down from twenty-nine minutes and fifty-nine seconds. Fifty-eight seconds. Fifty-seven seconds. After thirty minutes the microwave oven would start and heat up the can of soda. The numbers counted down like a ticking time bomb in a movie.

Because this was a bomb.

Cole looked into the living room; he watched Stella and David as they slept while he slipped his coat on. He could feel the stacks of money in his coat pockets that he'd stuffed earlier; the metal case of money, now about half full, still sat on the floor in front of his chair. He had also stuffed some packs of money into his socks and a few in his pants pockets. There was no way he could carry all of the money, but he guessed he must've had close to a hundred thousand dollars on him.

This was his share of the money, his mind whispered. And Trevor's. This was his starting over money.

At least he hoped he would have a chance to start over.

But first he needed to get out of this place alive.

Cole slid his hands into his thin leather gloves and he glanced at the clock on the kitchen wall. It was almost six o'clock in the morning.

And Frank and the others haven't even tried to attack yet, Cole thought. Why? What were they waiting for?

They are waiting for you, his mind whispered to him again. They are waiting to see what you will do, waiting to see if you will follow instructions and kill the boy.

Cole grabbed the flashlight he had set on the counter earlier and he walked as quietly as he could to the front door. He unlocked the deadbolt and the clicking noise sounded loud in the silent night, but he didn't even bother to turn around and look at Stella and David if they were waking up now. What could he do now? He didn't have the time to explain his actions or motives now because the clock was already ticking down to zero – down to detonation.

He slid the recliner out of the way and unlocked the door handle. He opened the door up to the freezing air, and then he slipped out into the pre-dawn darkness and closed the door behind him.

*

Stella opened her eyes and she watched Cole slip outside and close the door. It was a surreal moment for her as her mind drifted back to a similar scenario for her when she had slipped out into the night from the trailer at the dig site in New Mexico and ran outside for David.

She turned and looked at David. She thought about waking him up, but she didn't. Let him sleep some more; he needed his rest; he needed to be at his strongest in a little while when they made their escape.

She had read Cole wrong, she realized that now. She had believed that he was really going to stick around and help them. But she should've known better. He was a criminal and no matter how much he said he was going to change, he couldn't do it. He was still just a criminal.

She looked into the kitchen at the single dining room chair that was left. Cole had been sitting in it, she guessed, because one of the metal cases of money was on the floor. It was open, and even from here in the living room she could see that some of the stacks of money were gone.

She thought about taking some of that money. A pack or two could help her and David get far away from all of this.

She had decided not to go to her aunt's house. What would she do if this thing followed them up there? What would she do if it took her aunt and then sent her aunt back as a hollowed-out husk that asked for things in a gravelly voice?

Or maybe this thing would try a different approach next time. Maybe it would tear her aunt apart piece by piece; her aunt would scream and beg Stella to help her, to kill David so this thing would stop hurting her.

Stella closed her eyes for a moment and tried to push the terrible vision out of her mind. No, she couldn't risk hurting her aunt or anyone else that she knew. She needed some of that stolen money so they could run and find somewhere safe.

Stella got up and she hurried through the murky cabin and crouched down in front of the open case of money. So many stacks of money inside – one hundred dollar bills collected into a brick of money wrapped in plastic. Stacks and stacks of the plastic bricks of money. She was about to grab one of them, and then she thought of the old man who had been killed in the bank robbery. The one Cole said Needles had killed. This was blood money. A man had died for this money.

And many had died since then.

But she couldn't let that get to her, she needed to protect David, and she needed some of this money to take him somewhere safe, a place where he could grow up and become strong. Maybe she could find someone who could help them, a shaman or Medicine man who could train David to harness his powers.

That might mean going back to the Navajo reservation, back to where they had come from, back to where all of this had started.

But what else could she do?

She rolled up her pants legs and grabbed a few stacks of the money. She stuffed the money down into her socks and then rolled her pants legs back down to her hiking boots. She stuffed more stacks of money into the waistband of her pants. She took a few more stacks so she could stuff them into her coat pockets.

And then she glanced into the kitchen and saw the numbers on the microwave oven that sat on the counter. The numbers were moving; counting down.

And now she could smell the odor of gas coming from the stove.

And that's when she heard the thump from the freezer.

She jumped up to her feet and stared into the kitchen at the freezer against the far wall. The lid bumped again; it opened just a bit and then thumped back down.

"Oh God," Stella whispered.

CHAPTER FORTY-THREE

COLE STEPPED OFF the porch and his boots sank down into the snow. He had his gun in his coat pocket, but he didn't take it out; he wasn't even sure it would do any good anymore, yet he still felt better knowing that it was there.

He scanned the snowy field and the dark blob of trees with his eyes, but he couldn't see much in the darkness. The moon was already setting low in the sky behind the trees, but even with the scattering of clouds across the night sky, he could see a little bit into the darkness. He didn't turn on the flashlight yet, he would wait until he was inside the garage to use it. He didn't know if using the flashlight would attract this thing out here, but he had a feeling that it didn't matter either way – this thing knew he was out here now, he was sure of it; he could practically feel it watching him, waiting to see what he was going to do.

Waiting to see if he would follow instructions.

As long as Cole was following instructions, he felt sure that he was relatively safe for the moment.

Cole trudged through the snow towards the hulking black shape in the darkness that was the garage. He walked past Tom Gordon's pickup truck and it blocked the freezing wind a little. Already his face felt numb and his fingers were turning into ice blocks underneath his thin leather gloves. He paused for a moment at the end of the pickup and looked around one more time – nobody moving in the darkness. He looked back at Frank's spot in the snow, but Frank wasn't there. He looked back at the cabin which was dark except for the yellowish glow of the kitchen light in the windows. He didn't see any movement inside and the door wasn't open with Stella watching him from the doorway.

He turned back to the garage. He needed to hurry; he could see the digital numbers from the microwave oven (bomb) counting down in his mind.

He hurried through the snow to the garage doors which were already partway open from when he'd entered the garage days ago. But he would need to push the doors open even wider to drive the snowmobile out.

And what if it doesn't start? What if the battery is dead? What if that thing has known about the snowmobile the whole time and destroyed it already? What if it has known about your plans the whole time?

Cole pushed these thoughts away. He had to try. What else could he do?

He pushed at the other wooden door with his hands and immediately he felt the sting of the cold through his gloves. He pushed against the door, but it wasn't budging. He leaned into it more, driving with his legs, trying to find some traction in the scattering of snow on the concrete of the garage and the gravel of the driveway in front of the doorway. One last push, and he nearly screamed with effort as …

… the door broke free with a crackling of ice; the garage door let out a wail of protest into the freezing air as he slid it all the way open until it thumped to a stop.

That might have woken Stella, he thought.

He hurried into the darkness of the garage. It was like entering the mouth of a cave. He thought about looking for a light switch somewhere on the wall; if the electricity worked in the cabin, then it must work out here. But he didn't want to waste time with a search for the switch; he had to hurry. The flashlight should be enough to light his way. Besides, he knew exactly where he was going in the garage.

He turned on the flashlight, its beam knifed through the darkness and he could see the clouds of his quick breaths in front of his face. He moved forward through the pathways of boxes, crates, shelves, and junk. He came to the tarp over the snowmobile – it was just how he had left it, with a few boxes toppled down on top of the blue tarp.

Cole set the flashlight on a nearby shelf, and he tried his best to angle the light beam down onto the tarp. He pushed the boxes to the side and he ripped the tarp away; it made a loud crinkling noise when he stuffed it down between some boxes. He could see tiny ice crystals and dust floating in the air through the light beam.

And right where he'd seen it before was the snowmobile. He checked it over quickly, it was an older model, maybe ten years old he guessed, but it looked well-maintained. Living out here in the woods and mountains, this snowmobile would be someone's (Tom Gordon's) lifeline if a blizzard hit, and that person would take care of it; the snowmobile would need to be operable at all times.

He shoved his hand into his pants pocket and even though his fingers were beginning to go numb, he could feel the keys to the snowmobile. He grabbed the key and stuck it into the ignition. He twisted the key gently, he didn't want to start the snowmobile, he just wanted to see if the electrical system still worked and wanted to see how much fuel was in it.

The lights of the snowmobile lit up when he twisted the key, and he could see the fuel gauge – almost full. He twisted the key to the off position, took it out of the ignition and pocketed it. He didn't want to start the snowmobile yet – there was something else he needed to do, the other reason he was in the garage.

He grabbed the half-full gas can from the floor and ran for the open garage doors, he ran for the dark blue rectangle against the pitch black garage that was the open doorway. He almost expected Frank or Jose to step into that dark blue rectangle. He could see Frank's head cocked to the side in his mind; he could see that plastic smile. "Where are you going, Cole?" Frank would ask in his pleasant but gurgling and grave-cold voice.

Or maybe Trevor would step into the doorway.

Cole pushed the thought of Trevor away.

No one stepped into the doorway and Cole ran out of the garage and right to the cabin.

Frank and the others would be coming now, Cole thought. They would be coming when they saw what he was doing.

You're not following instructions, his mind whispered.

Fuck the instructions, Cole thought.

He ran through the snow as fast as he could and the gas in the plastic can sloshed as he stomped through the snow. His lungs were burning and his muscles were already aching from the run through the deep snow. He ran right up to the corner of the cabin, the same corner where Trevor had hopped over the porch railing down into the snow to check the back of the cabin the first day they were here – it seemed so long ago now.

Cole pulled off the plastic cap on the nozzle of the gas can and he tossed it into the snow; he wouldn't need it anymore, he was going to use every bit of this gasoline. He sloshed the gas all over the logs of the cabin. He ran down the side of the cabin, drenching the logs as he went.

He hurried around to the back of the cabin and he continued to douse the wood with the gas. But now he saw something in the darkness. Two figures stumbling through the snowy back field, stumbling right towards him. It was difficult to make out the details of the figures, but just by the awkward way one of them moved through the snow, like the pieces of his body were shifting against each other, and the tatters of clothing were hanging from the frame, he could tell it was Trevor.

Cole didn't watch them approach, he had to keep his mind on what he was doing, on his task at hand. The digital numbers were counting down in his mind. He rounded the corner of the

cabin and ran as fast as he could through the snow, still dous-
ing the logs on this side of the cabin with the gas he had left. He
was afraid Needles and Trevor would catch up to him. He was
afraid that he would feel cold dead fingers grabbing the back of
his neck soon, afraid that he would hear his brother's now-raspy
voice.

The gas in the plastic container was almost gone when Cole
got to the front corner of the cabin by the porch. He looked back
behind him; he could see his tracks through the snow, but he
didn't see the two figures anymore.

You know who they were, his mind whispered to him. They
were Needles and Trevor. You know that; don't try to pretend
that you don't know who they were.

Cole ignored the whisperings in his mind that seemed to be
getting louder and louder. He splashed what little gas he had left
all over the logs and then he threw the gas can into the snow. He
climbed up onto the railing from the snow and he clamored over
the railing and dropped down onto the floorboards with a thud
as snow spilled off his pants legs and boots. He got to his feet and
he was about to bolt to the front door, but a voice stopped him in
his tracks. It was Frank's voice – this monster's mouthpiece.

"What are you doing, Cole?"

Cole looked out at the field and he saw Frank standing in the
snow. Same Frank. Same clothes. Same smile. Same hollowed-
out body. Only this time Frank had someone else with him – Jose,
and Jose held an ax.

"You need to kill the boy, Cole," Frank said.

Cole took a step towards the front door, and then another, yet
he still kept his eyes on Frank and Jose.

As Cole took a step closer to the front door, Jose took a step
closer to the cabin.

Cole couldn't see Jose all that well in the darkness, but
even from what he could make out, he could tell that there was

something wrong with the way Jose looked, something wrong with his body, his neck, and his face.

Cole took another step towards the front door; he was only about six or seven long strides away from it.

And now Jose started running towards the cabin through the snow. He raised the ax up in his hands that were way too thin – almost skeletal.

Cole ran for the door. His boots clomped down on the floor-boards and snow flaked off of his pants and coat. He reached his hands out for the door handle as a thought raced through his mind.

What if Stella was awake now? What if she'd seen him leave? What if she had locked the door?

CHAPTER FORTY-FOUR

STELLA HADN'T LOCKED the door; she hadn't even made it to the door yet. She still stared at the freezer in the kitchen. She was on her feet now and she backed away from the nearly empty case of money and from the dining room table chair. She backed away from the kitchen with its microwave oven that she could see was clearly counting down numbers. She backed away from the smell of gas.

She backed away from the freezer. The lid continued bumping up and down, and then the lid finally crashed open and slammed into the log wall, held there by a thin arm with a spider-like hand.

Stella had backed all the way up into the living room, in front of the couch where David still slept. But she didn't look at David; she kept her eyes on the freezer where Tom Gordon sat straight up. His movements were jerky as he climbed out of the freezer, and his limbs, which seemed like they were at odd angles, popped back into place with loud snapping sounds as he moved. Tom Gordon's body wasn't completely thawed yet and the ice crystals still twinkled on his bluish skin. He stared right at Stella with his eyeless face.

And then he smiled.

"No," Stella whispered.

She finally turned to David. He was still sleeping on the couch, but his arms were straight up in the air and his hands moved like he was still drawing the symbols in his notebook, still writing an ancient language that he couldn't possibly know.

"David!" she screamed. "Wake up!"

David's eyes moved back and forth underneath his closed eyelids. Back and forth. Back and forth. But he wasn't opening his eyes, he wasn't waking up. His hands moved in the air as he drew the imaginary symbols.

"David!!"

She shook him. "You have to wake up!!"

A slamming noise startled Stella. She looked back at Tom Gordon who stood in front of the freezer on unsteady legs. But she realized the slamming noise hadn't come from the kitchen. It had come from …

… the front door.

*

Cole burst through the front door and then he slammed it shut. He locked the deadbolt, but he knew they were going to have to get out of this cabin very soon – it was a ticking time bomb.

"Cole!" he heard Stella scream at him.

He turned and saw Stella in front of the couch where David slept, but David had his arms raised up in the air and his hands were moving. But to Cole it didn't seem like his hands were drawing an ancient language in the air, to Cole it looked more like David was a puppeteer pulling on imaginary strings.

Cole saw Stella's eyes dart to the kitchen.

He followed her stare and saw Tom Gordon by the freezer, he watched him take a step away from the freezer, a step towards them.

"Where'd you go, Cole?" Stella asked in a cracking voice; she seemed close to tears.

Cole ran to Stella. "I've got us a way out of here," he told her. "Get David! We need to go!"

Just then something slammed into the front door – an ax. Cole snapped his eyes to the front door and he could see the tip of the ax poking through the wood of the front door. The ax blade wiggled out and it left a gash in the wood. A few seconds later the ax slammed into the door again.

Stella was watching the door as Cole grabbed her. "Get David up!"

"I've tried! He's not waking up!"

"I'll carry David," he told her. He saw that she had Jose's gun in her hand. "You need to put that gun down. You can't shoot that gun in here no matter what happens."

She nodded; she knew what the gas smell in the cabin meant. She dropped her gun on the floor, it landed with a thud.

Cole turned to bend down and scoop David up off the couch, but he never got the chance to pick him up.

"Where are we going?" Stella asked him

"We'll go out the back," he said, but even as Cole uttered the words he could hear the splintering of wood from down the hall, like something incredibly strong was tearing the back door off of its hinges.

They were trapped. They were surrounded.

It was never going to let you get out, Cole's mind whispered. It knew about your plans all along and it was always a step ahead of you. You were never going to outsmart it – it has been around a long, long time.

Tom Gordon stumbled towards them and he nearly fell on his unsteady legs, but he kept on coming, he kept stumbling towards them, impossibly seeing through the black holes where his eyes used to be. And he opened his mouth and bared his teeth in a rictus smile.

The ax hit the front door again and again. It had already nearly split the door right down the middle; the door was barely hanging in the doorway by the door handle and the hinges.

From the hallway, behind the flimsy barricade of the dining room table, Cole could hear two more bodies stumbling forward through the darkness.

Needles and Trevor, his mind whispered at him. Needles

with his eyeless face and the gory exit wound in his forehead that was now like another hole where a giant eye used to be.

And Trevor. Cole didn't want to think about seeing Trevor again.

Stella shook David again and again. She screamed at him to wake up. But he wouldn't wake up.

Jose split the front door apart with one last powerful strike from his ax. He stepped through into the cabin, into the light, and Cole could see Jose now.

The flesh from Jose's neck and throat were nearly gone; only a thin shaft of spine and a few spindly tendons held his head up, like some kind of flesh balloon being held aloft by a string of bone.

Jose's face had been peeled away in many places, revealing shiny white bone. On one side of his face, a large section of his teeth were visible now that the flesh was gone; his tongue flicked over the white teeth like a giant red slug.

Jose took a step towards Cole and Stella; he held the ax in hands that were skeletal, nearly all of the flesh had been torn away from his hands.

Cole and Stella huddled together.

Frank stood in the doorway and watched them. The thing out there was seeing through Frank's eyes, and it spoke through Frank's mouth. "Last chance," it said through Frank's mouth. "Kill the boy and we'll let you go."

Cole knew that he needed to get Stella and David out of the cabin now, in a few minutes the microwave was going to count down to zero and turn on. The can of soda was going to heat up and then it was going to spark and explode. And that was going to ignite the gas from the stove. And that was going to spread to the gas-soaked logs of the cabin outside. This place was going to become an inferno. He had to get David out of here; he couldn't let David die or all of his preparations would be for nothing. David would die. He and Stella would die. And maybe this thing wouldn't die – maybe it would go on living. David would be dead and that creature, that thing out there, whatever it was, would have won.

Cole couldn't let that happen.

Cole aimed his gun at Tom Gordon, then at Jose. But then he lowered his gun – it wouldn't do any good, one shot could ignite this whole cabin. Instead, he pointed his gun at himself; he shoved the barrel under his chin and laid his finger on the trigger, ready to shoot. He smiled at Frank.

"Move aside, Frank," Cole said. "You let Stella and David go or I'll kill myself."

There was a crashing noise from the hallway. Stella looked over and saw the dining room table thrown aside from the doorway to the hall. She saw Needles and Trevor stumble out from the darkness.

Cole wouldn't allow himself to look at Trevor or Needles – he kept his eyes on Frank. "Last chance, Frank," he said.

No answer from Frank for a moment, and then he cocked his head the other way and smiled at Cole. "Pull the trigger, Cole. Die. And then we'll all tear Stella apart with our fingers and teeth right in front of the boy. And you will help us."

Cole hesitated. He knew if he pulled the trigger there might be enough gas lingering in the room to cause an explosion. He couldn't risk it.

Something bumped into Stella from the couch behind her. She whirled around and saw that David was still asleep, but his body was levitating, floating up into the air; his body was already up to her shoulders. His legs hung down in the air, but his arms were still straight up, his hands were still moving frantically, still frantically writing.

Then the microwave dinged – the timer had counted down to zero. The microwave turned on and began heating the can of soda.

It was too late.

All of the dead men rushed towards Cole and Stella, even Frank. Their mouths were wide open; their hands were like claws now. Whatever parts the thing out there had taken from the bodies, it had always left their teeth – their gnashing teeth that could bite and tear at flesh.

Stella kept her eyes on David's levitating body as the tears rolled out of her eyes. "David," she whispered. "I'm sorry. I tried my best to protect you."

David's eyes popped open. His mouth opened wide, and he screamed.

"NOOO!! YOU CAN'T HAVE THEM!!!"

Sparks shot off the can of soda inside the microwave.

The dead men ran across the wooden floor of the cabin, they were almost on top of Cole and Stella. Cole kept his gun pointed under his chin, his finger still on the trigger. He'd rather die in the explosion than from their teeth.

There was a blinding flash of light.

A rushing of wind …

CHAPTER FORTY-FIVE

COLE'S EYES OPENED up and he could see a dark blue sky above him that was just beginning to lighten up from a rising sun somewhere still on the horizon in the east. But there was a light coming from somewhere else, a flickering light, a reddish-orange light. And the light was warm. A lovely warmth in the freezing cold.

But he couldn't hear anything except a high-pitched whine in his ears. Everything else seemed to be muffled.

He felt confused, unsure for a moment where he was, where he had been. He realized he was looking up at the early morning sky. He realized he was lying in the snow. And he realized that something near him was on fire.

The cabin.

The cabin was on fire.

Cole's sluggish mind struggled to remember as his hands and legs moved in the snow. He could feel the cold wetness of the snow saturating his clothes.

He sat up quickly and he saw Stella. She was only about ten feet away from him; she was sitting up in the snow. She might have been saying something to him, yelling at him, but he couldn't hear her.

She got to her feet and she ran over to something in the snow, a small dark shape slumped in the snow.

It was David.

Cole got to his feet and the high-pitched whine died away.

He could now hear the crackling fire from the blazing cabin. He could hear Stella screaming for David.

He rushed through the snow and he dropped down to his knees beside Stella as she shook David's body. She was crying; the tears spilled down her cheeks.

"Is he …" Cole asked.

David turned over in the snow and his eyes fluttered, then opened.

Stella burst into sobs and she hugged David. "Are you okay?" she asked.

He nodded and she picked him up into a sitting position on the snow. He smiled at her and he wiped away at her tears.

Cole looked back at the burning cabin. In the doorway and on the front porch were the burning bodies of what used to be his brother and the bank robbing crew. The bodies were being reduced to ash and bone very quickly in the blaze. A few of the bodies, now almost indistinguishable from each other, writhed and tried to move, but they were too badly damaged to escape now.

He could see something inside of the bodies – inside each one of them. It looked like something dark and leggy. The things slithered through each one of their ribcages, and then all of the things stretched out of the bodies and joined each other. The pieces of dark and slithery things formed a kind of a spidery creature that didn't make sense to Cole's mind; it resembled some kind of giant sea creature in the flames, like an octopus maybe, but the tentacles were jointed like a crab. And it seemed to be constantly changing form.

And then it scuttle/slithered deeper into the cabin, deeper into the fire.

Cole looked back at David who stared at him. "Did you get us out of there?" he asked David. "Did you save us?"

David didn't answer, he only stared at Cole.

"Yes," Stella answered for David. "He saved us."

Cole stared at David. "That thing … is it gone?" he asked.
"Yes," David answered. "For now."

*

Ten minutes later Cole had the snowmobile running. He drove it out of the garage, drove it past Tom Gordon's pickup truck, and then he came to a stop by Stella and David who waited for him. They needed to hurry – the smoke from the cabin was going to draw emergency vehicles eventually. And cops.

Stella got on the snowmobile behind Cole, and then she scooted back so David could climb onto the snowmobile in between them. She put her arms around David to protect him as they got ready to take off for the driveway that wound through the trees and joined the county road a half mile away.

She knew they were going to get away from this place, but she didn't know what Cole's plans were after that. She knew that she needed to get David to a safe place; she needed to find someone who could help David train, someone who could help David harness his powers.

Because this thing would always be after him – she felt certain of that.

Cole gunned the engine and they drove forward through the snow. Cole drove slowly, trying to be careful with all three of them on the snowmobile. Stella held on to David as he turned around for one last look at the burning cabin.

Stella didn't see the small and mysterious smile on David's face as he watched the cabin burn.

OTHER BOOKS BY MARK LUKENS:

THE SUMMONING

NIGHT TERRORS

ABOUT THE AUTHOR

I've written several books, many of which will be coming soon to Amazon and Kindle. I'm also an artist and a screenwriter. I live with my wife and son in Florida, not too far from Tampa. I welcome any comments or questions you may have.

Made in the USA
Lexington, KY
18 December 2019

58758579R00127